Desperately Seeking Pleasure

CHRISTOPHER MARKLAND

This is a work of fiction. Names, characters,
businesses, places, events, and incidents are
either the products of the author's imagination or used in a
fictitious manner. Any resemblance to actual persons,
living or dead, or actual events is purely coincidental.

Printed in the United States of America

Second Printing, 2019

ISBN-13: 978-0-9971230-1-2
ISBN-10: 0-9971230-1-X

Cover Design: Determined Books
Photography: Larry M. Newton
Cover Model: Danyelle Williams

www.DeterminedBooks.com
Facebook.com/determinedbooks
Email: books@determinedent.com

www.ChristopherMarkland.com
Facebook: Author Christopher Markland
Email: Christopher@determinedent.com

To my children: Brandon, Britt, Jay, and Hunt.
Thank you for inspiring me to keep being Determined

Stephanie, thank you. I love you!

Acknowledgements

To my mother, Jackie, thank you for your ceaseless encouragement, love, and support. Love you, Lady!

To Stephanie, thank you for your patience throughout the process of writing this book. I love you.

To my brothers and sisters—Lianne, Nikki, Kikki, Heidi, and Erick—even though we drift apart, we will always be close. I love you all.

Michelle, my editor and friend, thank you for your encouragement along the way.

To my friend, Elle "Fuego", not only has your help with this book been invaluable, but your friendship as well. My sapiosexual friend, IFWY!!!

From a turbulent international flight to a special friendship, Danyelle, thank you for being the friend that you are. Aries all day, your hustle and drive has motivated me to finish this book more times than you would even know.

Larry "Mike", you did it again. Without your vision, your eye, your passion, your talent, the cover for this book would never be. Thank you for putting your magic to the shot.

Thank you to my beta-readers, Erica, Bridgette, and Kiara for your honest feedback and criticisms.

To Boston, I followed your wise words to "Imagine that" the second book would be written, and look where we are now.

Thank you for reading this book. I hope you enjoyed it as much as I enjoyed writing it.

1

Dante

My mind was wandering anxiously as I juggled my shoes, belt, and backpack after scooping them up from the scanner. *Why did she want to take a cruise of all things?* I thought as I watched the bin containing my laptop, the last item that I was waiting on, travel down the conveyer belt towards me.

I was standing in the confined space of the security area in Charlotte Douglas International Airport in Charlotte, North Carolina. The steadily growing line of passengers being funneled through two of the three full-body x-ray scanners was not helping my already sour mood. Why they didn't have the third scanner working was beyond me. Surprisingly however, I made it through that part of the security screening process a lot quicker than I had anticipated. I was glad that ordeal was finally behind me because I was not fond of being in large crowds. It was something about being around all of these people, especially in such a small area, that made my skin crawl.

Walking over to the row of empty seats that were close by, I carefully negotiated my way through the other passengers standing by the conveyor belt waiting on their items to come out. As I sat down, I thought about how I had proposed several different ways that we could have spent our second wedding anniversary. She had vetoed them all for one reason or another—Vegas was too hot, Toronto was too cold, New York was too crowded, Los Angeles was too far, and she had already been to Chicago and had a bad experience on the flight there. When I suggested Miami, however, her eyes had lit up.

"Yes! Let's go to Miami," she said excitedly while a mischievous grin spread across her face. "And when we get there, we can get on a cruise ship and sail somewhere."

At the mention of the word cruise, my first thought was that I had absolutely no desire to be floating out in the middle of the ocean somewhere in a big hunk of metal with Captain Jack Sparrow behind the wheel. I felt that if God had wanted us to be out on the water, he would have given us gills instead of lungs.

She wasn't hearing any of that though, so here I was, stuck in this airport teeming with people all rushing here and there. Once again she ended up making the final decision as to what we would be doing and where we would be going.

Where the hell is she, anyway? I fumed, my annoyance building as I sat on one of the uncomfortable, gray chairs and scanned the security area, hoping to locate her. I stuck my foot into one of my shoes, and as I tugged it on, I saw a woman in her bare feet being pulled aside from the body scanner for a more thorough search.

"Please stand with your back to the wall facing me. Raise your arms, hold them out by your side, and remain still," the female Transportation Security Administration agent said in a firm, clear voice to the woman.

As other passengers gathered their items from the conveyer belt and prepared to make their way to their gates, I stopped what I was doing and watched the scene unfold. The pair were standing only ten feet from me. I could hear them both clearly and watched as the woman complied with the agent's commands and raised her hands as instructed.

The agent—a tall, attractive woman—quickly smoothed out her long, black ponytail so that it hung down in the center of her back before she began the pat-down procedure. She was light-skinned with a patchwork of small freckles on her nose and high cheekbones. A thick coat of lip gloss enhanced the moistness of her full lips.

She wore what appeared to be the standard issue TSA uniform, but hers seemed to be custom tailored, fitting every inch of her thick and curvy body. She stood in front of the passenger, which gave me the opportunity to check her out more closely. The navy blue pants clung to an ample behind, and even through the thick, polyester material, there was no missing the faint indentation of the lines of her bikinis underneath that were definitely not part of the regulations.

Her steel blue uniform polo shirt was doing its best to contain all of the abundant flesh underneath it. The position of the gold badge as it jutted out on the left side of her uniform highlighted how large her breasts were.

The agent ran her powder blue, vinyl gloved hands over each of the passenger's outstretched arms, starting at the fingertips and moving towards her shoulders.

The passenger was also an attractive woman in her own right. With pecan brown skin, she was slightly shorter than the TSA agent, which put her a few inches over five feet tall. She was wearing a simple black blouse and blue stretch jeans which accentuated her hips.

I don't know what it was exactly that held my attention, but I couldn't bring myself to turn away. I watched in increasing fascination as the agent's pat-down became even more thorough as she moved her gloved hands over the passenger.

I subconsciously licked my lips as I watched the agent work her way down the passenger's body, starting at her shoulders. The passenger's eyes, which had been closed up to this point, flew open as the agent's hands moved over her breasts. A soft sigh escaped her lips as the agent's hands lightly brushed over her chest as she examined the passenger's bra.

After hearing her exhale, the agent paused, appearing to study her closely. In that moment, they traded a brief but knowing look that seem to speak volumes. The agent quickly turned to her left, glancing in the direction of the other agents who were either going about their duties of watching the x-ray machines, moving the gray bins containing passengers' items through the conveyor belt, or standing by having idle conversation with each other. She then did a quick scan of the rest of the security area, checking each of the passengers. I quickly averted my eyes, pretending to fumble with my shoes, not wanting her to see that I had been covertly spying on them.

The agent returned her attention to the passenger, staring deeply into her eyes, a small smile playing at the corners of her mouth.

The passenger broke their long stare, turning away, her eyes also darting around the security area. Her gaze landed on me just as I had looked up to continue watching them. I was caught. I couldn't turn away as she locked in on me, a spy to their secret moment, looking at her.

Her facial expression changed as the realization that she was being watched sank in. We regarded each other for a long moment before she slowly turned away and closed her eyes.

The agent continued her pat-down, a change evident in the tone of the procedure. Instead of it being brisk, thorough, and almost clinical, there was definitely a softer approach to her actions. She moved her hands downward, tracing her fingers across the passenger's belly and downward to her voluptuous thighs.

"Spread your legs," the agent said in a whispered command.

The passenger nodded her head before opening her eyes, and complying silently with the directive, moving so that her feet were further apart from each other.

The agent lowered herself in a slow, deliberate motion. She moved into a squatting position until she was balanced on her haunches in front of the passenger.

The agent watched the passenger's eyes closely before putting a hand on either side of one of the passenger's thighs.

The agent slowly moved past the passenger's knees, down to her ankles, before slowly moving back up. As she came to the point of where she had started her movements, she continued up and stopped only when her right hand made light contact with the junction between the passenger's thighs.

At this soft touch, the passenger let out another soft sigh, a barely noticeable shiver coming over her.

The agent let her hand linger there for a brief second before shifting over to the passenger's other thigh. She repeated her movements, tracing her fingertips down the passenger's thigh, moving past her knees and down to her ankles. As she stopped there momentarily, she then continued to work her way up, this time moving even slower then she had before.

I stared at the passenger's flushed face, taking in her quickened breathing caused by the tantalizing tease of the agent's hand arriving at her body's midsection.

The passenger bit down on her bottom lip, standing there in the middle of the security area, her eyes closed. Her body slowly rocked back and forth as she tried to maintain her balance, arms still outstretched, holding a pose of sensual crucifixion.

Before the agent's hand reached the end of its provocative journey, she abruptly stopped. She quickly rose until she was standing fully upright, transforming back to her official capacity, the officer of lust once again becoming an officer of the law.

"Thank you, ma'am," she said, the authority evident in the loud, clear tone of her voice. "Please get your belongings. Enjoy the rest of your day and have a safe flight."

Without another word, the agent turned and went back to the area where the rest of her coworkers were assembled and joined them in conversation.

As if turning up the volume on a television that had been playing with the sound muted, the seemingly silent scene that had unfolded in front of me was now replaced with the familiar noise of the hustle and bustle of the busy airport.

I sat, dumbfounded, trying to understand what I had just witnessed. I tracked the movements of the passenger as she sat in one of the seats on the opposite side of the security screening area. Her head was down as she focused intently on fastening the strap on one of the black, platform high heels she slid on to her foot. I took in every detail about her, from the bright red nail polish on her long, elegant fingers to the matching color, vivid through the peep toe of her heels.

I realized that I was still holding on to my shoe, frozen still in the act of putting it on to my foot. I was sure the scene had taken at least an hour, but a quick glance at the large, digital clock in the middle of the airport concourse told me that less than two minutes had passed.

The woman finished buckling her shoes, picked up her purse and plane ticket, and stood to her feet. As I watched, it was clear that she was indeed a unique woman. Where all the other female passengers in the airport wore tennis shoes or other similar footwear, she instead was more akin to a runway model as she balanced herself on the three-inch heels. Strutting with a regal air of confidence, she walked away from me, sexily sauntering down the concourse.

I quickly slid on my shoe, grabbed my backpack, and trotted off to catch up to her.

"Hey! Wait!" I called out. I was a few paces behind her, but quickly closed the distance between us. "Hey! Hold up."

Finally drawing near to her, I reached out to take hold of her elbow.

"Yes?" she asked quietly, turning and looking up at me.

"What was all that about, Celeste?" I asked my wife, looking into her beautiful, brown eyes that always reminded me of pools of melted milk chocolate.

She was a complex woman, which oddly enough was one of the many reasons I was attracted to her. I had known her for almost four years, but what I had just witnessed a few moments ago was a side of her that I had never seen. *What the hell's going on?* I was confused, angry, and aroused all at the same time.

"What was what all about?" she asked, as if trying to deflect away my inquiry.

"That…back there…when you and her…you know what I'm talking about," I said, my frustration growing.

She closed her eyes as if trying to will her way out of the situation. Finally, she leaned forward and kissed me lightly on the cheek.

"I'll be right back," Celeste said. "I'll try to explain. I promise. But right now, I have to go get cleaned up." Without another word, she turned and headed off in the direction of the ladies' restroom, leaving me in a complete state of confusion.

2

Michal

Over the years, I had gotten used to people mispronouncing my name. I couldn't help but chuckle as the gate agent butchered it as she called for me to come up and see her. Instead of correctly pronouncing my name "Mih-Kahl," she instead was using one of the many different iterations that I have heard so many times before.

"Mee-Shall Sexton, please see the attendant at gate twenty-nine. Mee-Shall Sexton, gate twenty-nine, please."

My fingers were crossed in the hope that my request to be bumped up would be granted. I approached the counter just as she was putting away the handset and introduced myself. Reading her name off the tag on her shirt, I said, "Hi, Danyelle. I'm Michal Sexton. You just paged me?"

"Yes, ma'am," she said in greeting with a sympathetic smile on her face. "I'm sorry. I know you wanted to be moved up to first class, but the flight is completely booked."

"Thanks anyway," I said, turning away in disappointment. I returned to my seat in the gate twenty-nine area in the A terminal of George Bush Intercontinental Airport in Houston. I checked the time and saw that only a few minutes remained before it would be time to leave.

I resumed watching the ramp crew on the tarmac below go about their tasks of prepping the aircraft for departure. The flurry of coordinated commotion around the plane was absolutely fascinating to me. Several baggage carts were maneuvering around the fuel truck, which had been refueling the plane for the last ten minutes or so. A catering truck soon pulled up to the aircraft, extended the outriggers on both sides of the truck, and then rose upward over twenty feet until it was on the same level of the plane's fuselage. All of this activity was going into the flight preparations of the American Airlines Boeing 737-800, which would soon be taking me and all of the other passengers non-stop to Miami International Airport.

The clamor below blurred, my mind drifting off, as I thought about the weekend that lay ahead of me. The nervous energy coursing through me could hardly be contained. I couldn't wait to get to Miami and begin my adventures on my four-day cruise to the Bahamas.

Every two years, my girls and I would get together and take a 'Girlfriend Getaway' trip. I had an absolute ball on our last trip to Las Vegas with my long-time friends Kendra, Darlene, Maria, and Regina. I was starting to get excited as the memories of that trip mixed with the anticipation of the upcoming few days. I tried to stay patient but I felt myself getting antsy waiting for them to announce that we could board the plane.

The main point of our getaways was to reconnect with each other and to catch up on the events in our lives. However, unbeknownst to my friends, I used these trips as opportunities to set out on my own adventures. Our biennial excursions allowed me to leave my mundane life behind and pursue a few more interesting exploits.

I couldn't hold back the smile that spread across my face at the delicious promise of the things I would be getting into. Over the next four days, I had set three personal goals for myself, and I couldn't wait to get started on reaching them.

As I waited, I began to devise different schemes, imagining various scenarios and how they would play out. My thoughts were interrupted by a loud burst of static from the intercom.

"Ladies and gentlemen," the perky voice of the gate agent announced, "at this time, we will now begin boarding flight two-two-nine, service to Miami, Florida. If you are seated in Zone one, you are welcome to board."

I quickly pulled my curly, black hair into a ponytail and held it in place with a red scrunchie. Reaching down to pick up my overnight bag and purse, I made my way over to the gate. I joined the growing line of people that were poised like sprinters at a track meet waiting for the starting gun to give us the go-ahead to board the plane.

We waited patiently for her to finish her announcement and retract the belt into the stanchion blocking the door. After a short walk down the jetway, I was aboard the aircraft where I quickly found my row. After hefting my bag into the overhead storage bin, I took my seat and prepared for the flight ahead.

Just a few more hours to go, I thought as I pulled out a copy of Essence magazine. I glanced toward the plane's entrance and said the prayer that all passengers who get to their seat first say to themselves: *Please Lord, don't let this flight be sold out so that I won't have anybody sitting next to me.*

I sighed with relief when an attractive, middle-aged, woman wearing jeans and a bright pink tee-shirt promoting breast cancer awareness came to the row and indicated that she had the window seat.

I turned sideways in my seat to allow her to slide by me. We exchanged a few pleasantries before I returned my attention to my magazine.

Motivated by the article that I was reading on the importance of properly moisturizing dry skin, I took a second to pull out a small bottle of lotion from my purse, looking up the aisle as I did so. That's when I saw him enter. Well, actually, I felt him. I know it's a mechanical impossibility, but I swear that the front of the plane dipped about two feet when he boarded. As soon as I laid eyes on him, I closed my eyes and feverishly prayed to God, Allah, Jehovah, Yahweh, Zeus, or any other deity on duty at that moment that this guy would keep moving down the aisle and bypass my row.

Nope. No such luck. I studied him closer and couldn't believe that he was somehow sweating profusely from the daunting fifteen-foot road march from the front door of the plane to the row of seats where I sat. He paused for a second to catch his breath before finally wheezing out, "That's my seat," at the same time pointing a meaty finger at the empty middle seat next to me.

I glanced quickly at the lady in the window seat and we exchanged a look of horror at the situation in which we found ourselves. I have no problem with overweight people for the most part, but this guy had the audacity to get on the plane wearing a tank top that was letting it all hang out. I mean from belly fat to man boobs to arm wings, this guy was sporting the whole package.

I tried to stand so that he could get in to his seat, but before I could unhook my seatbelt, he had already started trying to squeeze his bulk around me. I pressed myself as far back into my seat as I possibly could, this deft maneuver saving me as his massive rear-end passed a millimeter away from the tip of my nose. In that frightful moment, I was exposed to the haunting sight of an enormous, pale white plumber's crack the size of the Grand Canyon. A pungent miasma that was a curious mixture of body odor and bacon aggressively invaded my nostrils as he passed in front of me. The odor caused my gag reflex to kick in and I wondered if this set of circumstances was the first of God's punishments because of my secret plans for the weekend.

After he was settled in, his bulk spilling over both armrests, I tried my best to find a comfortable position. The line of passengers that had backed up behind him as they waited for the aisle to clear finally started moving again.

I looked up and made eye contact with a handsome, coffee brown-skinned man wearing a light-blue shirt and blue paisley tie, the knot loosened casually. He had observed the entire scene and was shaking his head while wearing a big grin on his face.

As he walked by my seat, he leaned over and whispered into my ear, "I'll pray for you." The sugary sweet smell of the chewing gum on his breath helped to clear away the bacon-body odor smell that was still lingering in the air. He gave me an expression of pure pity while patting my shoulder before moving on to his seat.

Damn! Why couldn't he have sat next to me? I thought as I cut my eyes at the large mound of flesh beside me. It wasn't easy, but after several attempts of upper body contortions that would have made a Cirque du Soliel acrobat envious, I finally got comfortable and was even able to catch a quick nap. Before long, I was being gently shaken awake by the flight attendant telling me to prepare for landing.

After a smooth touchdown and what felt like the longest taxi to the terminal ever, we finally pulled into our gate and began deplaning. I powered up my iPhone and received the text alert that my girls were already waiting for me at baggage claim.

Let the fun begin, I thought as I picked up my things, quickly got off the plane, and went into the cool airport terminal. I could barely contain my excitement to keep from running through the terminal.

3

Celeste

We were making our descent into Fort Lauderdale–Hollywood International Airport just north of Miami, Florida. I had been looking out the window, however, the bright sunshine reflecting off the stark white of the dense, pillowy clouds surrounding the plane forced me to look away.

I sat with my forehead pressed against the thick plastic of the window, my thoughts and emotions whirling around inside me. Like the clouds enveloping the plane, my heart was shrouded by a thick fog of pain. My spirit was in turmoil, not only because of what had happened earlier in the airport, but more so with everything else going on with Dante and me.

As if that wasnt enough, I was also trying to deal with my fear of flying. As soon as the plane's door closed, my insides began to churn. That pain intensified even further as the engines powered up and we began rolling down the runway. My stomach had been in knots ever since take-off two hours ago and I knew that pain would stay until we touched down in Florida.

I turned my head away from the window and regarded Dante—my friend, my husband—sleeping peacefully in his slightly reclined seat. I loved him so much, but right now as he snored softly, completely oblivious to the angst that I was dealing with, I honestly didn't know how I felt about him.

This cruise was to celebrate our second year of marriage; however, our anniversary date was actually a week after we got back home. Although he didn't know it, this weekend would also be a major test for our marriage. I had so much tied up in the next four days, and the more I thought about it, the more it scared me to my core. I knew that I could have easily forced the issue a long time ago, but for now, things were solely in his hands. All I could do was hope and pray that he would make the first move, the right move. Here we were, about to celebrate a milestone in our marriage, but instead of being filled with joy and happiness, I was instead fighting back an overwhelming feeling of heartache.

Once again, I was second-guessing myself.. *Am I handling things properly?* I wondered. *Should I just go ahead and tell him what I knew and see how he reacted? Why was I even putting up with this situation with him in the first place knowing the crap I had been through in the past?*

I looked away from him in frustration. Trying to clear my thoughts, I focused instead on the dull gray of the shade covering the window, the bland façade mirroring my mood. My mind was a pendulum, my thoughts rapidly moving from my future dilemma and swinging to my past confusion.

I replayed the earlier interaction with the TSA agent in the airport over in my mind. An uncontrollable shiver raced through my body as I relived the encounter. I remembered the energy emitting from her clear, brown eyes. I could almost feel the soft, gentle touch of her fingers moving up and down my thighs. I shifted in my seat in an effort to tamp down the tantalizing tingle building within me. *Was this entire weekend going to be like this? Would I be able to control my behavior?* was the frustrating question that I asked myself as I threw up the shade and stared at the infinite sea of white nothingness outside.

After giving my eyes a few moments to adjust to the brightness, I took several soothing deep breaths, my mind slowly clearing and allowing my nerves to finally become calm. My thoughts drifted back to a conversation I'd had with my friend, an emergency room nurse at Presbyterian Hospital in Huntersville, North Carolina where we both worked. Earlier this week, we had been sitting in the cafeteria eating lunch together when out of the blue, she made a seemingly innocent comment about a patient. She told me about a patient that had been admitted earlier that morning with a knee injury. She went on to say that she was massaging the woman's leg and while having done this simple procedure countless times before, there was something about this one particular patient that had turned her on.

I was shocked at this admission, not only because of the randomness of the comment, but also at the fact that it was a glimpse into a side of her that I had never seen before. The next thing I knew, the conversation took a crazy turn when she opened up about her secret desires. I didn't know where any of that had come from. Granted, there had been times before where she had joked about being attracted to women, but that was the first time she had ever openly admitted this to me.

Reflecting on that conversation not only made me think about my interaction with the TSA agent in the airport, but also other times in my past as well. I had done so many things before but fought hard to keep everything pushed down, covered up, and locked away in the vault where I felt that it was best to leave them. Or so I thought.

The piercing chime of the 'Fasten Seatbelt' warning on the console above my head snapped me back to reality. A few seconds later, the plane's intercom crackled, indicating that the pilot was about to make an announcement.

This is it! We're about to crash, I thought, preparing myself for what I knew would be the pilot's final message to us before we plunged to our fiery deaths.

"Ladies and Gentlemen," he said in a reassuring tone, "this is your Captain speaking. We're flying into a little bit of choppy air. I've turned on the fasten seatbelt sign, so please remain seated with your seatbelt in place. We will be touching down in Fort Lauderdale in about twenty-five minutes. Thank you."

It took me a brief second to realize that "choppy air" was pilotspeak for turbulence. With that realization, the emotional anxiety I had been feeling up to that point instantly became mortal fear. As if a switch had been flipped, the aircraft began buffeting around, swaying left and right, climbing up and then dropping down what had to be several hundred feet at a time. I turned to Dante who had the nerve to somehow still be sleeping despite the fact that we were on the verge of utter catastrophe. *How in the hell could he still be asleep right now? Didn't this fool realize we were about to plummet to our deaths?* I wanted to grab him around his neck and shake him awake, but there was no way I could have done this considering the grip I had on both of my armrests.

The turbulence seemed to be getting worse. I just knew the wings would be ripped off at any second as violently as the plane was dipping up and down. At one point, the plane seemed to drop out of the sky, causing me to scream in pure terror. I reached over and grabbed Dante's hand, holding on for dear life. The contact of my hand on his somehow reassured me. That feeling was short lived however as we hit another pocket of rough air, which again made the plane dip and sway dramatically. Fear caused my hand to involuntarily close around Dante's, the force of my fingers crushing his like a vise.

"Ow! What the hell?" he asked groggily, waking up with a yelp and snatching his hand out of my death grip.

"The plane. The pilot said we're going through turbulence, but I really think we're going to crash and he just doesn't want to admit it," I answered, trying to speak calmly but doing a poor job of hiding my hysteria. I stared straight ahead, one hand gripping the armrest while reaching out and retaking his hand with the other.

"Huh? Crash? What?" he asked, sounding surprised and confused. He scanned the cabin, observing the other passengers seated around us on the flight, some reading, others napping, most engaged in quiet conversations with each other. He had flown with me before and knew all too well about my fear of flying, so I'm sure he had recognized the situation for what it was.

"Calm down, Celeste," he said in a soothing tone while reaching over with his free hand and using it to pry my hand off his. "We aren't going to crash. We're going to be through this in a few minutes. Okay?"

In my head, I knew that he was right, but the terror which was clutching my chest made it difficult to believe anything he was saying.

Oh my God! When will this flight end? I thought, squeezing his thigh as the fear rushed through me again.

Just as quickly as it began, the turbulence ended. The plane settled down, and the remainder of flight into Miami went smoothly. We were finally through the thick layer of clouds and I was able to see the lush green landscape below. As I watched the houses with their bright blue swimming pools in almost every back yard grow larger as we descended, I knew that in a few minutes we would be touching down. I looked forward to the moment that I would to finally be able to get off this manned missile and stand on firm ground.

With the turbulence behind us, I couldn't help but wonder if we would experience something similar during the cruise. I wasn't thinking about the ship itself sailing through rough waters, but more specifically the turbulence between Dante and me. The episode with the security agent had come out of nowhere, and I wondered if there would be similar issues like that over the days ahead. As much as I had prayed for nothing but smooth sailing, I felt we were off to a rocky start. Something told me that things were going to get worse before they got better.

4

Greg

I leaned forward so I could see through the tiny window beside my seatmate on my left. I was amazed at the clear blue sky which seemed to stretch on forever. The Delta Airlines MD-90 was cruising along at around thirty thousand feet above sea level and we were roughly halfway between the Hartsfield-Jackson and Miami International airports. With a little over forty-five minutes before we would be touching down, I was way beyond the point of no return.

I still wondered why I'd even made the decision to join my friends on this trip in the first place. It would have been so easy for me to have backed out, and nothing would have been said about it. To be honest, regardless of the fact that no one had actually said anything, I was sure everyone would have preferred that I didn't go.

Four days. It was bad enough that I would be trapped on a boat in the middle of the ocean with the woman who dumped me, but I was also going to be stuck out there with her new lover as well. *What in the hell was I thinking by putting myself in this position?*

The flight attendants who had been slowly making their way down the aisle serving snacks and beverages stopped at my row. I turned away from the window and thanked the tall brunette who served me. As I picked up the Sprite she placed on the lowered tray in front of me, I let my eyes wander around the crowded cabin of the plane.

I was crunching on a mouthful of ice as my gaze followed the aisle up to the activity beyond the opened blue curtain which separated first class from the rest of the plane's cabin. I took note of the difference in the level of service they were receiving up front compared to the rest of us. We were in the same aircraft hurtling through the sky at almost five hundred miles per hour; however, the sixteen people in first class had a much different experience than those of us who were seated in the economy section.

"Must be nice," I muttered dryly, raising my chin to point in the direction of the first class area of the plane.

"What is?" Evan, seated in the aisle seat in the row across from me, asked. He looked up from the audio stereo magazine he had been flipping through and took a sip from his cup before leaning into the aisle to peer into the first class cabin.

Evan Lucas was the youngest member of our group of six all currently in route to Miami. It was impossible to tell by the way he was slumped in his reclined seat, but he stood over six feet tall, had walnut-brown skin, a low fade haircut, and a thick beard that was his pride and joy. Possessing a quiet demeanor that belied his sarcastic wit, he was mature beyond his years and was a kind-hearted person. I was grateful to have him in my corner as both a friend and soon-to-be business partner.

"Check out the difference in service, E," I said to him. "See how nice they've got it up there in first class? They've got not one, but two flight attendants there to serve them. Two! Think about it; two people to serve sixteen and only three to serve the rest of us. That's crazy, right?"

"Umm…yeeaahh," Evan said in his trademark sarcastic tone, dragging out the word, all while rolling his eyes and shaking his head. He reached up and adjusted the nozzle for the air conditioning vent, took another sip of his drink, giving me one last sarcastic side-eye before returning his attention to the magazine.

"Evan, man, Mr. Thomas here knows damn well he isn't worried about first class seats or good service or any other such nonsense," Ethan said, leaning forward in his seat directly behind me to interject. "What he's really talking about is *who* is in first class. That's really what's bugging him."

Ethan Lucas, my best friend, was a few shades darker, two inches shorter, and seven years older than his younger brother, Evan. Whereas Evan was quiet, Ethan was borderline obnoxious with the silliest, damn near annoying sense of humor. Even with all of that, he was one of the realest, most genuine guys I knew.

He was seated in the aisle seat next to his girlfriend, Monica Langston. She had dozed off shortly after take-off and was lightly snoring. Ethan had put his issue of *Black Enterprise* aside and was listening to Evan and me talking. Having heard enough, he decided to add his two cents.

"Greg, we're going on this cruise to get away and relax," he said. "It's messed up that she's going with us and especially bringing ol' boy with her. But don't sweat it, man."

"Easier said than done," I said, turning slightly in my seat so I could see him over my shoulder. "You know the deal better than anybody else, man. This chick knew I was really feeling her and that I wanted us to be more than friends."

"I feel you, man," he said. "I honestly thought that she wasn't going to go with us after how things ended with you two. I know we invited her before everything went down, but she changed her mind at the last minute."

"Yeah, I know," I said derisively. "First she kicks me to the curb and then has the nerve to bring that bow-tie wearing, manscaping, metro-sexual motherfu—"

"Bruh!" Ethan said, reaching forward and putting his hand on my shoulder.

"I'm good, man," I said, taking a deep breath to try and calm myself. "I still can't get over that she got with him. And all because he has money? What kind of mess is that? Now I have to be stuck on a boat watching her and that fake, wanna-be Daymond John be all up on each other for four days?"

"Yeah, I understand. Seeing them together isn't going to be easy, man. Be cool though. Make the most of this vacation," Ethan said quietly as he gently pat my shoulder. "C'mon man.

You know she's Stacey's best friend, so she was going to be here regardless. Plus, keep in mind that this cruise isn't just about us. Think about him, okay," he said as he jerked his head backwards to indicate our friend who was seated behind him.

"I hear you, man," was all I could say, nodding my head in understanding.

Walter Johnson, who was in obvious pain based on the expression on his face, was trying to catch a nap. He had somehow managed to wedge his six feet, three inch frame in the narrow seat which was struggling to contain him. He was a big, muscular man, the results of years of weight training on display each time he moved his biceps.

The combination of his physique, height, and confined seating meant that the almost three hour plane ride would probably be uncomfortable for him even under normal circumstances. I was sure that uncomfortable was an understatement to describe his current situation. I was positive that he was feeling additional pain and discomfort, the result of the aftermath of the hours of surgery he had to undergo a few weeks ago to remove two bullets from his body.

His ex-girlfriend had shot him three times when she snapped after he ended their two-year relationship. Only one of the bullets grazed him; however, the other two hit their target, doing extensive damage to his left arm and shoulder.

Watching him, his face occasionally creasing with a grimace as the pain shot through him, I knew that no matter how intense my emotional pain was, the physical pain that Walter was going through was that much worse.

Finally, Walter moved around before settling down and laying his head on the person next to him. Stacey Twiggs, his new girlfriend, had her window seat reclined and was taking a nap. She adjusted her position instinctively, allowing both of them to find comfort in the cramped confines of their seats.

Watching this scene of love and affection play out in front of me, I realized sadly that Ethan was right. The source of my irritation was the two people comfortably seated together in first class. The more I thought about it and as much as I hated to admit it, not only was I resentful of my ex and her new boyfriend, I was also jealous of all my friends coupled up on this trip.

I wanted that. I wanted what they had. I thought I had stumbled upon the exact same thing with the developing relationship with her, but instead the woman that I had fallen in love with was now sitting twenty feet away from me beside another man.

5

Dante

It felt so good to finally be outside and able to breathe fresh air. I grinned at Celeste who had lost the battle with Florida's intense humidity which had relentlessly attacked her hair, causing it to become a frizzy mop on her head.

"I'll be right back," I told her as I turned my attention to the long row of taxis. The cabs were all parked along the curb outside Miami International airport, waiting to pick up their fares.

"Where are you going?" she asked distractedly, her attention focused on putting her unruly hair up into a ponytail.

"I'm gonna get us a ride," I said over my shoulder as I walked towards the taxis.

After several negotiation sessions, I was able to work out a deal with a driver to take us directly to the port for ten dollars less than any of the other drivers. Celeste and I had planned every aspect of this trip for months, budgeting to have fun without worrying about our household finances.

Lord knows I had to make sure my money was right because with everything I had going on back home, I had to squeeze every penny until Abe Lincoln cried for mercy.

"I got it worked out," I said as I walked over to the bench where Celeste was seated waiting for me to return. "Dude said he'd take us to the port for only forty bucks."

"That's good," she said without much enthusiasm as she stood and picked up her purse and carry-on bag.

Getting the rest of our luggage, I brushed off her tepid response and led the way to the cab.

"This is my wife, Celeste," I said, introducing her to the driver as I put down our bags by the tailgate of the SUV.

"Good morning, Ms. Celeste," the driver said as he held her door open. "Welcome to Miami. It's my pleasure to drive you and your husband today."

I don't know what happened, but Celeste seemed to freeze up as soon as he spoke to her. She just stood there, staring at him in confusion.

"Celeste? Baby? You okay?" I asked, gently putting my hand on her forearm. This was the second time today I'd witnessed her going into whatever strange place her surroundings were prodding her to go. This trip was off to the craziest start and we hadn't even made it to the ship yet.

"Hel...hello. Thank you," she said hesitantly, finally coming out of her momentary trance and climbing into the back seat of the truck.

What's going to be next with her today? I thought as I went around the truck and climbed in beside her. First, the scene in the airport, and now this.

Our driver radioed in to his dispatch that he was heading out with two people before he turned up the volume on the radio. The music, a classic reggae song by the world famous Jamaican icon, drowned out the sounds of the busy airport. Listening as he implored his woman to not cry, I couldn't help but smile at how perfectly the song's quiet energy fit our current mood.

As we merged on to the highway connecting Fort Lauderdale to Miami, I glanced at Celeste. She had been staring out the window at the passing scenery and I wondered again what was going on with her.

We drove along, neither of us speaking; the only sound in the vehicle coming from the radio. Taking my cue from the lyrics of the song where the singer repeated the refrain to his muse that everything was going to be alright, I took her hand in mine and said, "Celeste, I get the feeling that I'm going to be asking this a lot this weekend, but is everything okay?"

"Yes, I'm fine. The driver just reminded me of someone, that's all," she said, turning to me briefly before returning her attention back out the window.

"I've never seen you act like that before," I said. I wondered who could have made such an impact on her to have caused her to literally stop in her tracks. There was no similarity between our driver's voice and her dad, uncles, cousins, or any of the male family members that I have interacted with. "Who did he remind you of?"

"Jonathan," she said simply.

"Who's Jonathan?" I asked. There had never been any mention of anyone by that name. My heart was pounding, my senses on full alert, my curiosity completely aroused as I waited on her answer.

Turning back to me, she gave a weary smile before asking cryptically, "I guess you have to give honesty if you want to get it, right?"

"Huh?" I asked, even more confused than ever.

She let out a long sigh before speaking again, "Before I moved to Atlanta to attend nursing school, I was living in Augusta, Georgia and going to college there. That's when I met Jonathon. He was older than me and was a sergeant in the unit my dad commanded at Fort Gordon. Anyway, he and I had been together for about a year before my dad was transferred to Fort Bragg in North Carolina. With all of my family gone, I stayed in Augusta to finish school and of course, to be with Jonathon. That didn't last long because before we knew it, he had orders to go to Korea. Long story short, a month after he left, I found out I was pregnant."

"What?" Dante gasped in surprise. "Pregnant? What the hell?" I couldn't believe this. "Why didn't you tel—" I began, but stopped midsentence. I couldn't bring myself to ask her that question knowing that I had my own set of issues to deal with.

"Why didn't I, what?" she challenged, whipping her head around, staring directly at me with a scowl on her face.

There was something unnerving about the way she asked the question. I quickly pushed that thought aside and focused on how I could change the subject.

"Umm...why didn't you tell me about him before?" I asked, smoothly pivoting away from her question.

"He never came up before now, that's why," she snapped, her aggravation with me clearly evident. "And since it didn't have anything to do with you, I kept my past where it belonged—in the past. Well, I tried to anyway."

I sat back in my seat and let her words sink in. It seemed I was learning more about my wife in the last couple of hours than I had over the last few years. I knew that she had things in her past she hadn't shared with me, but I couldn't help but wonder what else was still hidden.

My past was far from squeaky clean and I didn't know if I could ever bring myself to reveal the secrets that I was keeping from her. *Maybe now was the time for me to unload the dinosaur sized skeleton I had hidden in my closet,* I thought as I closed my eyes.

I took a deep breath and said, "You're right, Celeste. And speaking of the past..." I paused and gathered my courage.

"What about the past?" she asked in an annoyed tone.

"It's just that I—"

"We're here," our driver announced, his voice booming in the relatively quiet interior of the Suburban as he brought the vehicle to a stop. "Let me get your doors for you."

I opened my eyes and was shocked that we had arrived at the port. I was so focused on my thoughts and the conversation with Celeste that I had lost track of everything around me.

I looked in amazement at the huge ship docked against the port. I knew that now would not be the right time to share something so devastating with Celeste. Not right as we were getting to leave.

"You know what, baby?" I said, using my most upbeat and jovial tone. "I'm just being dramatic. Like you said, the past needs to stay in the past. We're here, so let's have fun in the present."

Celeste silently regarded me for a few moments before rolling her eyes and saying, "Whatever, Dante."

This weekend was for us to enjoy each other and I was going to make sure that we did just that. Having kept my secret for this long, there was no reason I shouldn't be able to keep it a few more days. I just hoped that Celeste wouldn't reveal any more of her past because I wasn't sure where that would lead us.

6

Michal

My heart filled with joy as I approached my girls who were lounging around the baggage carousel. Regina, Maria and Kendra were preoccupied with their phones all the while having animated conversations with each other.

After graduating from Texas Southern University in Houston more than a decade ago, we'd all moved to cities in Texas and Georgia in order to start our careers in our chosen fields. As is usually the case, we settled into our own lives, our professions, got married, had children, and slowly drifted apart from each other. Weekly phone calls became monthly, dwindled to yearly, to finally none at all.

As the social media revolution picked up momentum, we found ourselves reconnected with each other. We not only caught up on lost time, but we were able to stay in contact with each other on a daily basis. We made a pact that no matter what, we would get together every two years for a girlfriend's getaway trip.

As I scanned the group of beautiful black women, I loved how we were all in our mid-thirties and looking damn good. We each had the confidence that comes from growing into yourself and knowing exactly who you were and what you wanted.

Regina Dawson was a woman who carried her size twelve, milk chocolate complected body with extreme self-assurance. She was as sophisticated as always; her hair set in a stylish, asymmetrical bob with frosted auburn tips. She was proudly showing off pictures of her two young children to Maria Gonzales who was standing next to her. Maria, a curvy Puerto Rican, with straight jet-black hair tied loosely in a ponytail draped over her shoulder, was laughing at something Regina was saying to her.

The last member of our group, Kendra Washington, my roommate for the cruise, was a tall, heavy-set, coffee colored woman with a shy smile and quiet demeanor. Or at least she used to be heavy-set. I did a triple-take when I saw Kendra, as I didn't recognize her at first glance. She used to weigh over 250 pounds, but it now seemed as if she had lost half of that weight since the last time I saw her.

Unable to stay quiet any longer, I had to let them know I was there. "HHHEEYYYY!" I screamed. The sound of my greeting caused them all to turn and gape at me before getting up and rushing over to engage me in a huge group hug.

After we had calmed down, there was an awkward silence for a few minutes. I could tell that we all wanted to say something about the fifth member of our group who was not with us, but none of us knew how to broach the subject. I couldn't find the words and honestly, now wasn't the right moment to bring it up anyway.

"How long have you guys been here?" I asked instead, breaking the tense silence.

"About an hour," Maria answered as she helped me grab one of my suitcases off the carousel that was rapidly filling with luggage. "I caught an early flight," she continued, as she struggled with the heavy suitcase.

"I've only been here about thirty minutes," Kendra said.

"Me too," Regina chimed in.

"Cool. Well let's get to the ship! I am so excited," I said as we headed out to catch a shuttle to take us to Port Miami.

"Kendra, I think we might have a problem," I said as I took measure of the inside of the narrow closet in our stateroom. "I don't think we're going to be able to fit all of our stuff in here."

There was no way our ocean view stateroom could be confused with a suite. I wasn't sure of the exact dimensions, but between the both of us, there wouldn't be enough closet, drawer, cabinet, and counter space to store all of our clothes, shoes, undergarments, cosmetics, and the many other things that we had brought along for the trip.

"You might be right," she said as she peered over my shoulder to see for herself at just how narrow the closet was.

"I guess I could leave some of my dresses in my suitcase," I offered. "I'll use half of the hangers and you get the other half. That's really the only way to make it work."

"Yeah, we really don't have many other options," she agreed dryly.

We were silent for a few minutes as we busily went about unpacking and setting up our personal items. I finished up and flopped onto my bed.

I bounced up and down to test the softness of the mattress and noticed that Kendra, who had finished unpacking, was now staring out the room's oval shaped window.

"Girl, you know I'm impressed, right?" I asked, trying to engage her in conversation. She had been friendly for the most part, but she seemed to be kind of distant with me.

"Huh? What are you talking about?" Kendra asked, glancing back over her shoulder at me.

"Your weight loss, that's what," I said, tossing a pillow playfully at her. "Don't try to be all modest. You know exactly what I'm talking about."

"Stop it!" she yelled sharply, angrily swatting the pillow across the room. She scowled at me before turning back to the window and directing her sudden outburst of anger towards the blue waters beyond the thick glass.

I was completely taken by surprise by the intensity of her response. "I'm sorry," I said meekly, trying to understand how I had provoked that reaction from her.

She took a long, deep breath before responding in a much calmer tone, "I didn't know what you meant, that's all. I wasn't being modest, but thank you."

"You really do look good though," I continued, still trying to get over my shock. I had only been trying to pay her a compliment because for as long as I had known her, she had been on the heavy side.

"Thanks," she mumbled, her back still to me as she continued watching the water.

I got up from my bed, trudging through the thick fog of tension that had settled in the room, and picked up the pillow from where it had landed. Not sure what to do next, I moved over to the small sofa by the entrance of our room and sat down, holding the pillow in my lap, silently waiting on her to make the next move.

"It hasn't been easy," she said, turning and facing me directly, her face still wearing a mask of pure contempt. "It has taken a lot of discipline to get here. I had to change everything. I changed what I ate, when I ate, how much I ate. Everything."

"How much have you lost?" I asked warily, wondering if her earlier outburst was due to me commenting on her weight loss. I was careful to pick my way through the conversation in order to prevent any more angry outbursts.

"So far, I've down 93 pounds," she said. "When I started this new program, I weighed in at 262 pounds. That was right after our last trip."

"Really? You've been going at it for two years?" I asked in surprise.

Kendra and I used to talk regularly, but for some reason, our conversations had all but ceased. Except for a few Facebook posts here and there, we didn't communicate with each other like we used to.

"Yes, that's right," she said wryly. "Two years ago on our last Girlfriend Getaway. Let's just say that I saw something that really motivated me."

As she said this, her eyes narrowed into angry slits. I was taken aback by how intense her feelings were but was still bewildered as to where it was coming from. Only a few minutes ago, I had been feeling light and happy, but now I was in a state of utter confusion.

"I saw something when we were in Vegas that really shook me up. Or should I say pissed me off," she said, turning away from me, her facial expression shifting from one of contempt to absolute disgust.

"Really?" I asked, trying to tamp down the nauseating feeling I felt rising inside me. "What did you see?"

"Oh, you know what I saw. I saw you and—" she began, spinning her head around to face me right as the ringing of the stateroom's telephone interrupted her. She moved to answer it, speaking briefly to the person on the line.

"That was Regina," she said, her eyes shifting away from mine. "They're up on the main deck waiting on us."

Without another word, she got up and went into the bathroom and closed the door behind her.

Oh my God! I thought as I sat on the sofa and blew out a long breath. I reviewed all of the things that I had done in Vegas and my heart skipped a beat as the details of certain memories came flooding back. I got up from the bed and went over to my suitcase, hoping and praying that Kendra was not referring to what I thought she was.

7

Celeste

As soon as we made it to our stateroom, I tossed my handbag on the bed and ran out onto the balcony. Leaning over the railing, I watched as jet skis and other vessels, small and large, motored by on the deep blue water of the port. Our room was on the starboard side of the ship so we were able to see out beyond the bay, all the way out to the horizon. This made for the most spectacular view as the sun shimmered on the water.

I enjoyed the tableau in front of me and felt my body, my mind, my spirit, all finally calming. It seemed that from the time we'd left our house in Charlotte this morning, there was one thing after another for me to deal with. From the pat-down in the airport security area, to the cab ride to the ship, no sooner had I thought that I was getting into a good place mentally, something else would happen to unsettle me and pull me back down. I wanted to leave all of the negative energy behind at the port and practice being positive and happy for the rest of our anniversary vacation.

"Baby, come and look at this view!" I squealed as the realization that we would be sailing out shortly filled me with excitement.

I glanced back over my shoulder at my husband, my heart fluttering as I watched him get up off the small sofa and come over to join me. Lately, my spirit usually ached when I saw him, but he still never failed to stimulate my body. No matter what had happened or how things might play out in the future, there was no denying that Dante, standing six feet tall with smooth, light brown skin, a low fade haircut, and a neatly trimmed goatee, was a sexy man.

"Wow, this is nice," Dante agreed as he stepped over the threshold separating our room from the balcony. A broad smile spread across his face as he stood beside me and took in the view.

"I know, right?" I agreed. "I'm so glad we did this! I can't wait to finally head out."

He took me in his arms. "Yeah, me too, baby." Gazing into my eyes, he pulled me close to him. "I'd be lying if I said a cruise was something I wanted to do, but checking out this view, so far this isn't too bad. A few of the guys at work had told me how nice the experience would be, so I was a little curious about this cruising thing. I'm still not crazy about being on the water for all that time, but we're here now so it's all good."

"You didn't want to go on the cruise?" I asked, surprised to hear him telling me this. Throughout the whole process of planning our anniversary trip, Dante had never said anything about not wanting to go. This was just something else on the long list of things that he was keeping from me.

"No, not really," he said. "I told you that when you first came up with the idea, remember?"

I was silent for a few minutes as I processed his words. I thought back, searching my memory. I drew a blank, not recalling him saying he wanted to do something different.

"You probably don't," he continued with a chuckle, releasing me from his hug and turning to lean on the railing. "You were so caught up with the idea that you didn't hear anything I had to say about it. At that point, I just said whatever and went with it. I love you, so if you're happy, then I'm happy."

With our arms touching, the body contact comforting, his words reassuring, we silently took in the peaceful scene before us.

Watching the activity on the water below, I realized why I had wanted to go on a cruise. Not only did I need to get away, I also needed to do something exciting. Nothing extreme like skydiving or mountain climbing, but something that Dante or I had never experienced.

My mind had been so jumbled lately that there were many nights that I couldn't even sleep. I needed this trip so badly that last night, I had been like a kid on Christmas Eve. Maybe that was the reason I lost control earlier in the airport with that TSA agent. I closed my eyes as I again thought about her touch. I bit my bottom lip as I recalled her hands and how they moved gently over my body. Her voice, her touch, the entire moment took me back to places and times I thought I would never revisit.

I shook my head to clear the memory from my mind, once again feeling myself getting caught up in that moment. I had to maintain self-control because there were so many things that Dante didn't know about me. There were too many unanswered questions and unresolved situations from my past. This trip was not the time for me to unleash those secrets. I had withheld so many things from him over the past two years but until the right time came, I would continue to keep them locked away.

Two years of marriage. Every time I stopped and thought about it, all I could do was shake my head in disbelief. After everything that had happened with Jonathan and the crazy years that had followed him, I never thought I would be able to find real love again, much less be married. There were times at work when I stared at my left hand and marveled at the gorgeous wedding set symbolizing our union.

My mind drifted back to that wonderful spring day in March a little over three years ago when Dante came to my job at Presbyterian Hospital in Huntersville under the guise of him taking me out for lunch. I bent down under the nurse's station to get my purse and when I stood back up, there he was, down on one knee right there in the middle of the cardiac ward. In his outstretched hand, he presented me with a spectacular 1½ carat, flawless solitaire diamond ring. My coworkers were in tears as they witnessed his proposal to me.

"Celeste Walls, will you do me the honor of being my wife?" he had asked, surveying me with nervous sincerity. "Will you marry me?"

As I silently stared at him and then at the ring that sparkled almost obnoxiously under the bright overhead lights, all I could do was cry. I was at a complete loss for words as the emotions churned inside me. Feelings of happiness, excitement, fear, shock, relief, and so many others all fighting to be expressed at the same damn time.

"Dante, I...I," I began, trying to speak but the words couldn't make it through the big, goofy grin that covered my face.

"I tell you what, Dante. If she don't hurry up and give you an answer soon, you can come over here and ask me, okay?" the head nurse quipped, breaking the anxious silence that had settled over the small group gathered around us. Up to that point, everyone had been caught up in the romance of the moment, silently awaiting my answer to his proposal.

"Yes, baby! Yes! Yes! Yes!" I said, almost screaming with joy as the weight of what my words meant washed over me. All of the other nurses and hospital staff members who had been witnesses to his proposal all exploded with cheers and clapping at my enthusiastic answer.

Dante stood to his feet, took the ring out of the box, and slid it on to my waiting finger. It was a perfect fit, just as he was a perfect fit for me. A year later, we were married and now, here I was, Mrs. Celeste Wright, celebrating my second wedding anniversary on what I prayed would be the most romantic cruise ever. I wanted us to enjoy not only all of the amenities and activities that the cruise offered, but more importantly, I wanted us to enjoy each other. I wanted us to use this time together, just him and me, no outside distractions by family, friends, our jobs, or anything else that would divert our attention away from each other. The next few days were going to be fantastic and we were going to make the most of them. The end of the year was right around the corner and we might not get many more chances like this again.

I snapped back to reality when I heard Dante's voice.

"This is pretty cool, baby. I have to admit," he said quietly as he turned to face me and pulled me close to him, gazing deeply into my eyes. "This was a great idea and I'm happy to be here. With you. I love you, Celeste."

I leaned into him and allowed myself to be lost in his words, lost in the moment. I raised my head and moved forward to kiss him, the world ceasing to exist the second that our lips touched.

Wrapped in his strong embrace, we kissed for what seemed like hours. When we finally broke away, he continued to hold me close, my head on his chest. Appreciating the warm fragrance of his cologne, this feeling of being close to him was so powerful, I loved every intoxicating moment of it.

"Come on, baby," he said as he took my hand and led me back into the room. "Let's go make this boat really rock."

"Hey now!" I giggled as he lifted me off my feet as soon as we got inside the room. I wrapped my legs around his waist and kissed him as he carried me straight to the bed. These were the moments I could see myself letting go and forgetting everything. Almost.

8

Greg

I had just unlocked and pushed the door open when Evan shoved by me, dropped his bags in the doorway, and dove headfirst on to one of the twin beds. I stood at the threshold and watched him do his impersonation of an Olympic high jumper as he flew across the room before flopping down on the bed furthest away from the room's entryway.

"Finally!" he said, kicking off his Jordans and rolling around on the crisp, white linen.

"I feel you on that one," I said as I collapsed on the tiny couch and propped my feet up on one of the armrests.

"Man, we've been on the go all doggone day," he said, clasping his fingers together behind his head which was propped up by two thick pillows. "I got up this morning, caught the train to the airport and had to wait there for two hours. Then we get on the plane, only to have to sit on the runway for another hour before spending another two hours in the air only to finally land to Fort Lauderdale.

Then we had to ride in that hot, raggedy shuttle van to Miami for another hour to get to the port."

"Don't forget having to stand in line for over an hour to get checked in before we could even board the ship," I said dryly.

"Exactly! Hell, after all that, I'm exhausted. And we haven't even left the dock yet!" he added in exasperation. "I'm gonna need a week off to recover from all the work that goes in to going on vacation."

"True. It's been a long day," I said, leaning forward on the couch so I could focus directly on him. "I've got a question for you though."

"Yeah? Whattup?" he asked, sitting up on the bed and facing me.

"How you just gonna take that bed like that?" I asked, making sure to keep a straight face as I spoke. "I mean, damn! How you know I didn't want that particular bed? You didn't even ask before you hopped your happy ass on it and claimed it."

"Whatever, dude," he said, squirming his slim frame around in an obvious attempt to show not only how comfortable it was, but also to stake his claim even further. "Man, you ain't back in the joint. *You is free now.* So, you can keep all that 'bed check, homie!' stuff on that side of the room," he said as he pointed to the empty bed.

"Damn! If you and your crazy brother don't act just alike." I said, shaking my head at the fact that Ethan and Evan shared the same warped sense of humor. Evan was more laid back than his high-energy brother but his sarcasm could cut deeper than the sharpest knife. Despite knowing both of them for so many years, they definitely kept me on my toes whenever I hung out with them.

They were also amongst the small minority of people that knew about my felonious background and that I had served jail time for an armed robbery conviction. Back in those days, I was a hardheaded thug—quick tempered and ready to square up and do battle at the drop of a hat, no questions asked. My actions in the streets caught up with me, but luckily I was only judged by twelve, instead of being carried by six.

The years that I was locked away in the state penitentiary matured me, teaching me that there was more to life than crime. I grew and developed more during that time than I had in all the years prior to the cell doors being slammed shut. After getting out, I promised myself I would never end up in that position again.

"While you're playing though," I continued as I inspected the small room that was going to be our home for the duration of the cruise, "this room's about the size of the cell I was in. Damn near the same size, for real. The only difference is that I can go in and out that door whenever I feel like it."

Evan got up from the bed and picked up his bag from where he had dropped it when he made his enthusiastic entrance into the room. "This is actually a lot bigger than I thought it would be."

As much as I hated to admit it, I knew that he was right. We were in what was actually a pretty good sized room, all things considered. The pain and anger that I was feeling was causing me to gauge everything associated with the cruise in the most negative light possible.

"But you're right about one thing though," he continued as he placed his suitcase on the bed and began to unpack its contents. "We're going to be stuck on this boat for the next four days and once we leave the port, there aren't too many ways we'll be able to get off. There's the off chance that we might run into an iceberg somewhere between Miami and the Bahamas. Well, maybe not. I don't think icebergs are in season yet. Other than that, you might be able to leave the room, but you're still basically trapped on the ship until we hit the port."

"For sure," I said, nodding my head in agreement but silently praying for one of those icebergs so that I could use one of the lifeboats to escape. "So, that means that while we're on this floating prison, we need to make sure we have some fun, right?"

"Yes, sir! Now you're talking like you got some sense," he said with a laugh as he reached out his fist to me.

The room's phone began to ring just as I gave a pound to Evan's fist.

"Whattup?" I said as I answered the phone. "We were just talking about you, Ethan."

"I'm not quite sure I like the fact that two dudes alone together in a tiny room are talking about me, thinking about me, or anything in between," Ethan said. "Before you even offer, the answer is NO. I do not want to join in whatever games you two are up there engaged in."

"What do you want, man?" I asked, shaking my head at the fact that I would be out on the open water with this fool and his brother for the next four days. It was going to take a lot of patience. And alcohol.

Through his laughter he said, "We're going up to the Lido deck in a few minutes to chill and watch the ship pull out. Y'all coming?"

"Yeah, that's wassup. We'll meet y'all up there," I said, relaying the plans to Evan before ending the call.

After getting our cell phones, key cards and sunglasses, we left the room and headed towards the elevators at the rear of the ship.

"You okay being on here with Angel? I mean, you'll have to see her and her dude every day. You gonna be cool with that?" Evan asked.

I had been thinking about that the minute I got to the airport in Atlanta and saw them there together. Cory was now the person that Angel, the woman I had fallen in love with, was dating. There wasn't anything that I could do about it. At the end of the day, things were the way they were for a reason. If she and I were supposed to be together, then so be it. If not, I was fine with that as well. Either way, I was going to be okay.

"You know what, E," I said as we turned the corner and entered the elevator lobby, "yeah, I'm good with it. She's obviously doing her, so I'm going to do the same thing and do me."

We stood in a small crowd of people who were talking excitedly amongst themselves as they waited on the elevator. As we waited for the elevator, I took a moment to admire the Oriental-inspired lobby. The area was opulent with its soft lighting, vivid colors, highly shined surfaces, and rich wood paneled décor.

The elevator arrived and Evan and I boarded. We stood along the back wall as the elevator ascended before coming to a stop on the Verandah deck, allowing more passengers to get on. As the doors slid open, my mouth dropped allowing a quiet "Damn!" to escape when I caught sight of a woman getting on. She had a body that looked like it was ripped from the scenes of a rapper's music video. She wore tight denim shorts that were more like a second skin the way they hugged every inch of her curvaceous figure. Her upper body was showcased in a short T-shirt, which stopped right at her navel allowing the perfect view of a toned stomach accented by a diamond piercing in her navel.

I would still be staring at her if I hadn't noticed the expression of the guy getting on the elevator behind her. There was no doubt they were together and a quick glance at both of their ring fingers confirmed this to be so. He underscored their relationship when he gently pulled her closer to him.

Caught red-handed staring at her, I quickly averted my eyes toward the polished reflective steel of the elevator ceiling. As attractive as she was, disrespect wasn't my style. If the roles were reversed, I wouldn't want anyone to try me. That didn't stop me from stealing a few more glances at the two hams she had managed to smuggle aboard the ship by hiding them in her shorts.

If she was an example of the women that would be on this cruise, then things might just work out better than I could imagine. It would definitely be lot easier to forget about Angel than I thought. And, I would damn sure have fun doing it.

9

Dante

The elevator doors slid open silently, finally allowing us to step out of the cramped space. It seemed like everyone on the ship was heading to the Lido deck at the exact same time. Celeste and I were amongst throngs of other people, all excitedly heading out to watch the ship leave the port signaling the official beginning of the cruise.

I was a step behind Celeste as we went through the sliding glass door leading outside from the ship's darkened interior and into the bright Miami sunshine. I couldn't help but notice the stares Celeste was getting from the men while we searched for an empty deck table.

It became tiresome to see some of them trying to surreptitiously check out my wife and sneaking glances at her behind. On more than one instance, I had to make eye contact with a few guys, literally staring them down when their ogling had lasted a bit too long.

It was always the same regardless of where we went. It didn't matter if we were in church on Sunday or out eating in a restaurant, these clowns gawked in amazement at my wife's physical attributes, damn near tripping over themselves to eyeball her. They would recover from the daze her body had put them in and quickly look over at me to see if I'd caught them checking her out. Then they would awkwardly avert their eyes until we moved past them.

The two guys in the elevator a few minutes ago did that exact thing as soon as the doors opened and they laid eyes on Celeste. The big guy's jaw almost hit the floor and I'm sure I wasn't the only one that heard the 'Damn!' that he said under his breath when he saw her.

Why does she have to wear outfits like that? I thought watching her plentiful rear end jiggle with each step she took in the pair of daisy duke shorts that she was wearing.

Her generous bosom was barely contained in a pink baby doll T-shirt emblazoned with 'Keep Calm, I'm A Nurse' across her chest. The only piece of clothing she had on that could remotely be considered conservative would be the brown leather gladiator sandals on her feet.

We found an open table and quickly claimed it. Judging from the big smile on her face, Celeste was in a good mood for a change. I relaxed in my chair, not trying to hide the grin that spread on my face as I silently applauded my performance in the room earlier which I was sure was the reason for the smile on her face.

Sitting back and observing her, I was again struck by how much I loved my wife. With her radiant smile, sensual curves, and bubbly personality, I was awestruck by how beautiful a woman she was. The problem was that everyone who saw her outside of the scrubs that she wears to work can also see just how beautiful she was. That was because her wardrobe consisted of tight-fitting pants and low cut blouses, or both.

The more I sat and thought about it, the more annoyed I became until I just couldn't contain my silence any longer. "Why did you pack that outfit in the first place?" I blurted out as soon as the waiter who had just taken our drink orders left.

Upon hearing my question, the smile that had been plastered on her face up to that point faltered before disappearing altogether.

"What? Are you serious right now, Dante? We are on a cruise, right?" she asked in a loud, sarcastic tone. "I'm wearing shorts and a T-shirt. What do you suggest—a polka dot dress that stops at my ankles? You want me dressing like Madea out here? Is that what you want?"

"No, baby. I don't want that at all," I said, instantly kicking myself for not keeping my mouth shut. I didn't want this to turn into a bigger argument than it was already shaping up to be. "I love your body, and Lord knows I could stare at you all day. I just get tired of all these dudes staring at you whenever we go out in public because of the outfits that you have on, that's all."

"If you liked the way I dress so much then why the hell did you—" she snapped before catching herself midsentence, her eyes narrowing into slits as anger suddenly darkened her visage. She slammed her eyelids closed for a few seconds before she spoke again. "Dante," she said in a much quieter tone. "I love you and only you. I wear what I want to wear because it's my body and I don't care who stares at me. As long as they don't disrespect my man, my marriage, or me, I don't care what anybody does. I can't believe we're having this argument again and that we're having it now."

I was caught off guard by her initial reaction. She had tried to temper her words, but I was still struck by what she had said. *Why did I do what?* I asked myself, wondering what she was going to ask before she stopped herself.

"I know, Celeste," I said, sighing with resignation. "I don't want to argue either. I just couldn't hold it in anymore."

"It seems that you have a real problem holding things in, Dante," she said with a sneer, turning her head away.

"Huh? What does that mean?" I asked, my heart falling into the pit of my stomach.

"Nothing, Dante. Don't even worry about it," she said with a hint of sadness in her voice as she turned back towards me.

I was totally lost at how things between us had gone from good to bad in a span of minutes. But this had become the normal routine for us lately; one minute we were as close as two people could be and the next, we would be bickering over the slightest thing.

"You know what?" I asked, hoping to lighten the mood and get us back to the happy place we had been enjoying before things went south. I leaned forward and reached over to take her hand. "It doesn't even matter, baby. I love you. All of you, with your sexy self. I just get a little upset and to be honest, a little jealous of the attention you get. I deal with it most of the time, but for some reason it really bugged me today."

Celeste squeezed my hand reassuringly before getting up and coming over to me. She sat on my lap and gave me a big hug and kiss.

"Dante Wright, you are the only man for me," she said, holding my face in both of her hands and looking directly into my eyes, emphasizing her words. "I love you and only you. I want you and only you. You are my husband, and I am your wife. No matter how I might dress or what I might do, it doesnt matter to me. If you do what you're supposed to do, then there isnt anything or anyone that can come between us. No one. Ever."

I took in her heartfelt words. Here we were, getting ready to sail out on a cruise to celebrate the anniversary of our marriage but I was once again letting other people get in between my wife and me. You would think I would have learned better by now. I had allowed enough people to get between us and a few dudes staring at her were the least of them.

Her words replayed on a loop in my mind, and I thought about the fact that she was indeed the only one for me. I knew in my heart and mind that this was without a doubt the truth. My body on the other hand was so weak. *How could I have been so stupid?* I thought to myself, the same question I had been trying to avoid once again invading my thoughts as it had done so many times before. I shook my head, trying to push away that nagging question. I knew we would have to talk about that later. If I could find the courage to do so, that is. The question could hopefully wait a few more days, a few more weeks, until we were back at home before it could be addressed. For right now though, I was at peace and that was good enough for me.

"I love you, too, Mrs. Celeste Wright," I said, leaning over and kissing her gently on her soft, full lips. It felt so right, so good, that even the loud blasts from the ship's horn didn't stop me from enjoying our passionate kiss.

10

Greg

The sound of the powerful air horn reverberated throughout the port, signaling that the cruise was finally about to be underway, and bringing a loud cheer from the crowd gathered on the deck. There was truly no turning back for me.

Evan and I had caught up to the rest of our group and we were leaning on the rail watching the dockworkers below finalize the ship for departure. They had just removed the huge blue ropes holding the boat to the dock and with that, we were ready to set sail. A few moments after the horn sounded, the ship's motors powered up almost violently, causing the ship to shudder briefly. Slowly, we pushed away from the dock and within minutes, moving down the wide channel, heading out to sea.

It was a gorgeous, sunny day, making it hard to believe it was November. If things remained like this for the duration of the cruise, then maybe my decision to go wouldn't be such a bad one after all.

Although I had originally made plans for Angel and I to go together, everything changed dramatically the night I went over to her house to go over the plans for the cruise with her. She tried to deal with the fact that we wouldnt be flying first class, but after learning that we would'nt be in a balcony stateroom like the other couples, she was done. Right then and there, she ended her our relationship.

Gazing out at the Miami skyline in the distance through the smoke tinted lenses of my sunglasses, I lamented that I was once again alone. I believed that after many years of searching for that one special woman to be in my life, I had finally found that person in Angel. I hoped this cruise would have been a romantic opportunity for us to get closer to each other, but here I was instead, alone.

Listening to the water slapping against the ship's hull as we slowly sailed through the harbor, I reflected on how much my life had changed over the last sixty days. From losing a love to winning a lottery, It felt as if I had pretty much done it all.

I chuckled to myself as I thought about the day my coworkers bought those lottery tickets for me. I still couldn't believe that a chance play of five dollars in the Georgia Lottery Fantasy Five instantly turned into $200,000 when the quick pick numbers that were selected matched with the winning numbers.

Evan, a successful entrepreneur who was a car and home audio installer, had been kicking around the idea of moving out of the shared space that he was currently renting and buying his own shop. The only thing stopping him was finding the right business partner. With my lottery winnings sitting in my bank account, I went to him and discussed us working together. After a short conversation to go over the details, we cemented the deal on the spot with a handshake. We decided to go on the cruise not only to support Walter, but to celebrate our new partnership as well. He was not sure who he wanted to take with him and ultimately decided to go alone and use the time away to relax.

My friends were all standing around me and inevitably, my eyes settled on Angel. I was again amazed that I would be sailing out into the deep blue ocean with my ex-love and her new beau with only the space of the huge ship to separate us.

What did she see in that clown? I thought as I observed the two of them together. Angel's new man had his arm wrapped around her, pulling her close to him. I shook my head to clear the memory of the first time I met him. Ethan, Evan, Walter, and I were hanging out at a restaurant celebrating Walter's break up with his crazy ex-girlfriend. We were having a great time when in comes Angel with him in tow. It was bad enough just seeing her with Cory, but to make it worse, she had lied and told me she was going out with her girlfriends that night. I would never forget seeing the deer-in-the-headlights expression on her face when she saw me sitting in the restaurant and knew instantly her lies had caught up to her.

I didn't know what he did for a living, but whatever it was, he had plenty of money and didn't mind throwing it around. When Ethan told me that Cory had paid for both is and her first class plane tickets from Atlanta to Miami as well as their junior suite on the cruise, it just further cemented my dislike for him.

The more I learned about him, the more tempted I was to pick up his super tight white slacks rolled up at the ankles, blue Hawaiian luau shirt, boat shoes with no socks, Kangol cap, aviator shades wearing behind and toss Mr. Pretty Boy over the railing.

I was still debating whether I should use a one or two-handed toss when Ethan stepped away from the railing. He called out to us, held up his Mai Tai, signaling he wanted to propose a toast.

"That's a pretty fruity drink you have there, sir," I said, causing the group to break into laughter. "I mean, damn! You've got your pinky all tooted up and everything."

"Why are we friends?" Ethan asked, the big grin on his face negating the earnest tone of his question.

The laughter died down and he took a long appraisal of each of us before speaking.

"I wanted to thank all of you for coming out," he said. "These last few months have brought us joy, love, pleasure and pain. I'm so glad that we're here on this Thanksgiving weekend, to give thanks for everything we have. We're truly blessed to be alive, to be healthy, to be able to love, to be loved. We've been through some tough times and I know our love and friendship will see us through whatever rough times lay ahead. Cheers!"

"Cheers!" we replied in unison, raising our glasses and joining him in the toast.

Angel's man pulled her in close and gave her a long, loud, wet kiss. *Yes, indeed. He's going overboard just as soon as we get into deeper water,* I thought as I watched him sloppily kissing on the woman that only a few weeks ago I was holding close to me.

"Let's go check out the rest of the ship," Evan said, coming out of nowhere and grabbing me by the arm and leading me away from the group. I guess he saw my face and wisely pulled me aside.

"You okay, man?" he asked when we were out of earshot from the group. "You looked like you were about to do something real crazy back there."

"I thought I'd be cool, man," I said in frustration. "But watching them together is going to be harder than I thought. I don't know what I was thinking by coming on this damn cruise knowing I still have feelings for her."

"Well, there's nothing you can do about it now," he said sadly. "Unless you're gonna be like Cullen Jones and swim back to the dock, you're going to have to deal with it for the next few days. I can't tell you how, and it damn sure won't be easy, but you have to find a way."

We spent the next few minutes mingling amongst the large group of diverse people gathered across the sprawling expanse of the Lido deck. The atmosphere was festive as everyone enjoyed the sunshine and excitement of the moment.

We passed by a table where four attractive women sat together, sipping drinks, engaged in conversation. I caught the eye of one, and we sized each other up for a few seconds before a small, almost imperceptible smile spread across her face. There was something about the way she regarded me with electric intensity, practically measuring me. She nodded her head slowly and then took a sip of her drink, all the while still maintaining eye contact with me. After putting the glass down, she licked her lips sensually before breaking our stare and returning her attention to her friends.

I continued walking and as we moved away, I wasn't sure what had just happened, but I felt both intrigued and aroused at the exchange. Something told me I would be seeing her again and she might be just the distraction from Angel that I needed.

11

Michal

After fighting through the masses of people on the crowded deck, we finally spotted Regina and Maria sitting at a table on the other side of the ship.

"Glad you decided to join us," Regina said with a laugh when we approached them. "You owe me for coming out here early and locking down this table."

I was just about to respond when I was interrupted by the loud, unexpected sound of the ship's horn blaring out three long blasts. It startled me so much, I almost jumped out of my skin. The raucous cheer from the crowd further surprised me so much so that I thought my heart was going to beat out of my chest.

"Jesus!" Regina shrieked, putting her hand over her chest and taking a huge gulp of her margarita.

After we all regained our composure, I told Regina, "This is a great spot. Next drink is on me, okay?" I said, giving her a high five across the table before taking my seat. I stopped one of the passing waiters and purchased a drink from the tray that he was carrying.

Scanning the large crowd of people gathered on the deck, I watched a muscular guy and his friend as they walked by our table. I checked him out, my eyes drifting over every inch of his body. I smiled to myself, pleased with what I saw. He must have felt me looking at him because he turned to look at me and our eyes locked for a long moment. I put my full lips on the tip of the straw and took a long pull of the drink.

I enjoyed the taste of my Sex On the Beach, savoring the cool libation on my tongue. *He might do just fine,* I thought before swallowing the sweet concoction and then turning away from him.

As the alcohol began to relax me, I took a second to appreciate the relief of being out of the tension-filled room and outside in the fresh air. It also helped to have the buffer between Kendra and myself that was provided by having our other friends as a distraction as well.

"And now that everyone is finally here, before we go any further, let's make a toast," Regina said.

Satisfied we all had our drinks, Regina held up her glass and said, "To all of my girls, those who are here and the one that isn't. To good times, good fun, good friendships."

"Cheers!" we all said, tapping our glasses together before taking sips of our drinks.

I enjoyed the taste of my Sex On the Beach, savoring the cool libation on my tongue before swallowing the sweet concoction.

"I just can't believe what happened to Darlene," Regina blurted out suddenly, as if not being able to hold her emotions in check any longer. "It's so sad." Her eyes filled with tears.

The fifth member of our group, Darlene Quarry, was a peculiar woman to say the least. She was beautiful physically, having been blessed with a flawless, honey-colored body. Tall in stature, standing five feet nine inches, her forceful personality made her seem even taller. You could feel her intensity whenever she locked her piercing, brown eyes on you. It was as if she were gazing into your soul, and to say it could be disconcerting was an understatement. Over time, I got to know the real person and every time I thought about her, I couldn't believe she was dead.

"I know," I agreed, reaching over and gently rubbing Regina's back. "She was my roommate back in college and was like a sister to me. She wasn't the warmest person to be around, but she was still a good person."

Kendra's eyebrows flew up in surprise and an expression of disdain flashed across her features. She quickly composed herself and took a sip of her Piña Colada as she turned away from me. I wasn't sure if anyone else noticed her reaction because I probably would have missed it myself if she hadn't been sitting directly across from me. More curious to me was why my comment had even caused her to react in that manner. I knew that sooner, rather than later, we would have to finish the conversation we started earlier. I had worked too hard to keep certain things under wraps, but it seemed Kendra knew a lot more than she was letting on which was very unsettling to me.

"I still don't even know what all happened," I continued, trying to push back my concerns about Kendra. I would dig deeper into things when I got her alone, but for now, this moment was about our lost friend. "I called down to Atlanta to talk to Darlene when she hadn't responded to the update we sent out last month. I couldn't get in touch with her, so I ended up calling her brother. That's when I found out what happened. He said she died in a car accident after getting into an argument with her ex-boyfriend."

"Ex-boyfriend?" Kendra asked in surprise. "When I spoke to her six months ago, she said they were engaged to be married next year."

"Nope. Ex-boyfriend. And it was more than just a simple argument that led up to her dying in the car accident," Maria said, putting down her apple martini and sitting back in her chair.

We all sat in confused silence, staring at her, mouths agape, waiting for her to explain further.

"When you called and told me she had been killed in a car crash," Maria said, looking at me, "the cop in me wanted to get all the details of the accident. I called one of my contacts, a detective with the Dekalb County Police Department there in Georgia, and he filled me in."

"Okay? So, what happened?" Regina asked, leaning forward in her seat.

"Well," Maria started, sitting up in her chair and taking another sip of her drink. "It turns out that she and her boyfriend had broken up a week before the accident. In fact, he had actually kicked her out of the apartment they had been living in together."

"Damn, he kicked her out, huh?" Kendra sneered, using her hand to cover a smirk. Kendra and Darlene had never been close friends. I knew the rift between them was formed by comments made about Kendra's weight back when we were in school and their relation had never improved over the years since.

"Yes, girl, he kicked her out," Maria continued, interrupting my thoughts. "But this is the crazy part; the same day she died, her ex and his friends had moved her into a new apartment. It turns out she still had a key to his place, and went back later that evening and shot him."

"Shot him!" I said, my hand reflexively coming up to cover my mouth.

"Yes, ma'am. Shot. Him," Maria said, spacing out her words dramatically before taking another sip of her drink. "Three times in fact. He didn't die though. He was hit twice and they dug a third slug out of a stud in the wall. That last one only grazed him."

"What was his name again?" Regina said, snapping her fingers together in an effort to remember Darlene's boyfriend's name. "Was it Wallace? Warren? No, it was Wilber, right?"

"Nope, his name was Walter. Walter Johnson," Maria corrected. "I had to find that out from the report my friend sent me. She rarely said his name whenever she talked about him, if she even mentioned him at all."

"I know, right?" Regina asked, nodding her head in agreement. "She was so secretive when it came to him. It's almost like she didn't trust us or something. It was weird how she did that, but I just chalked it up to another one of Darlene's quirks."

"She probably had a good reason not to trust some of y'all conniving witches around her man," Kendra muttered under her breath, her words barely audible over the loud music being played by the live calypso band entertaining the large crowd gathered on the deck. But I had heard every word, however, and my eyes flew wide as her statement registered with me.

Oh my God! Please tell me that she doesn't know about that too! I thought frantically as I stared directly at her across the table. She turned her head as if purposefully trying to avoid making eye contact with me. The evil grin now permanently plastered on her face let me know that she was well aware that her words had hit their mark. With each snarky comment and facial expression, there seemed to be no doubt that Kendra knew a lot more than she should have. No matter how difficult the conversation would be, I was going to find out exactly what she knew.

We spent the next few minutes quietly sipping our drinks and taking in the scenery as the ship slowly sailed through the Miami harbor, but I was beyond distracted by Kendra's antics.

Regina suddenly turned and said to Maria, "Wait a minute. I get that she shot him, but how did the car crash come about? Was she running from the police or something?"

"Kinda-sorta," Maria answered in that relaxed tone of hers. "They figured that she was trying to flee the scene and that's when she ran a red light. She chose the wrong time to do that because a semi-truck slammed right into her. She died at the scene."

I was horrified listening to Maria tell the gruesome details of Darlene's untimely death. She recounted the facts of the report where they had to pull her mangled, lifeless body out of the twisted wreckage of her car.

After she finished speaking, I sat back in my seat and reflected on just how precious life was. In a strange way, I felt validated in my personal quest that I was on for the cruise. I knew life was short and when it was your time to go, there was nothing you could do about it. I enjoyed a good, happy life in Houston, but on these getaways, I allowed myself to live outside the margins. I smiled to myself as I thought about how much living I planned on doing over the next few days and nothing, not even Kendra, was going to stop me. Life was indeed too short, and I was ready to live it to the fullest.

12

Greg

I struck several GQ model worthy poses as I checked myself out in the long mirror in our stateroom, smiling with satisfaction at the handsome reflection I saw there. I knew I was looking good in my baby blue linen trousers and matching vest over a starched white shirt with French cuffs held in place by a pair of sapphire blue cufflinks.

"Damn, are you done yet? You've been all up in that mirror like a woman for the past ten minutes," Evan said as he cinched the complicated Eldredge Knot on his blue tie around his neck. He was pretty dapper himself in his grey slacks and black vest over a royal blue shirt.

"Jealousy is such an ugly thing. Don't let it consume you," I said as I turned back to face the mirror to give myself a final once-over. "I tell you what I'm going to do; when we get back home, I'll give you some fashion tips so that one day, you might be able to look half this good."

Evan rolled his eyes so dramatically that I thought they would pop out of his skull. "Man, let's go," he said, shaking his head as he passed me on his way towards the door.

I spritzed a shot of cologne on my neck before following him out of the room. Our timing was perfect because Ethan and Monica were making their way from their room heading in our direction.

They made quite the attractive couple in their coordinated outfits. Ethan, his bald head freshly shaved and gleaming in the overhead lights of the hallway, had on black slacks and a sea foam green vest over a black shirt with green crystal cufflinks. Monica looked magnificent in a strapless, sea foam green dress with a black sash cinched around her waist, accentuating the black, suede heels she wore.

"GT, you look like the University of North Carolina mascot in that get up," he quipped while checking out my outfit as they came up to where we were standing.

"I swear, both of y'all Lucas boys are filled with hate tonight," I replied. "Like I told your brother, when we get back to the 'A', I'll give both of y'all lessons on how to be as upscale as I me."

"No, thanks," Ethan said, taking a long look at my footwear. "Wearing shoes made out of the skin of the Geico gecko is not my idea of fashion."

"Sir, these shoes cost more than your entire outfit," I said, lifting my foot to showcase my baby blue gators. "This is grown man wear. You wouldn't know anything about this."

"No argument there because I don't plan on getting to know anything about that," Ethan said, shaking his head as he took Monica's hand in his. "Let's go, y'all. The rest of the crew is already downstairs at the table waiting on us."

We made the quick elevator ride to the fourth deck and were met with groups of other similarly well-dressed people. Before long, we filed inside the huge, multi-level Lincoln dining room and were escorted to our table by a hostess.

"Looking good, Stace," Ethan said as we took our seats around the table where Walter and Stacey were already situated. "I'm surprised you could find an outfit large enough for King Kong over there."

"Oh, Lord. Here we go," Walter groaned.

"How long did it take you to shave him, anyway?" Ethan continued, never missing the opportunity to tease Walter about his size. No matter how many bullet holes were in him, Ethan was going to get his digs in regardless.

"Ethan, don't you start. My baby doesn't have time for your foolishness, okay?" Stacey warned, a smile on her face as she wagged her finger in his direction.

I had to agree with Ethan; Stacey was indeed looking good tonight. She had on a simple black dress that stopped mid-thigh. Her legs were encased in black stockings decorated with an elaborate pattern showing off her thick, shapely thighs. Walter was also well dressed in a blue slacks with a grey vest over a grey shirt and matching blue tie.

"Okay, okay," Ethan said, raising his hands in surrender. "Where's your girl, anyway? Are they coming down?"

"I don't know where they are," Stacey said. "She said they were on their way down. That was thirty minutes ago. I thought they'd have been here by now."

"It takes a minute to get all the way down here from the penthouse suite," I said, trying to hide the derision in my voice, but wholly unsuccessful in my attempt.

"Chill out, man," Evan said as he plucked one of the freshly baked dinner rolls from the breadbasket our waiter placed in front of him.

"Speak of the devils," Stacey said, pointing to Angel and Cory who were coming in through the dining room's entrance on their way to the table.

My heart skipped a beat when I saw her. She was absolutely breathtaking in a form fitting, dark purple cocktail dress, which showcased just how sexy she was. I had to force myself to look away so I wouldn't stare at her. No matter how hard I tried, I couldn't get over the hold this woman had on me.

I turned back to look at them and had to do a double-take when I saw the outfit Cory was wearing. I wanted to laugh, but all I could do was shake my head in disgust. This fool had on a European cut suit with pants so tight, it seemed as if he had on black leggings. I was sure that his nuts needed a rescue air tank because they had to be starving for oxygen. I glanced at his feet and couldn't believe he had on suede loafers with pink tassels, matching his pink bow tie.

Something was off with this dude. He was put together way too trendily for my liking. I couldn't put my finger on it, but something about him didn't quite sit right with me.

"Hello, everyone." Cory said cheerily, pulling out his chair and sitting down. Angel had paused by her chair, I assumed to give Cory the opportunity to pull it out for her. Seeing that this wasn't going to happen, she quickly recovered, pulled it out for herself, and sat down beside him.

The next hour was spent with good conversation and delicious food. I was enjoying my second helping of steamed lobster tails with lemon butter sauce and listening to Monica talk about her business, Sweet Sinsations, which specialized in alcohol-infused cakes and cupcakes. She currently had shops in both Decatur, Georgia and New Orleans, Louisana and was making plans to open a third location in one of the cities in suburbs north of Atlanta.

Our waiters were busily moving around the table refilling our glasses and restocking the table with fresh bread. Angel took that opportunity to reach for one of the baguettes in the basket in front of her. Cory reached over and firmly put his hand on her forearm to stop her.

"You've eaten enough tonight," he said simply, not even bothering to look directly at her. He focused instead on the dessert menu the waiter placed on the table in front of him. He spoke in a patronizing tone, as if she were a misbehaving child.

Obviously embarrassed, she meekly withdrew her hand, reaching over instead to pick up her glass of water.

How in the world did a woman as strong as Angel allow herself to be handled the way that he was treating her? I thought as I looked across the table at both Angel and Cory in amazement. I was trying to understand what the hell had happened to her in the short time that she had left me to be with him.

Cory put down the menu, took a sip of his wine, and we locked eyes across the table. I knew he could see the fire in mine, but as I stared into his eyes, I saw nothing. No emotion. No feeling. Nothing.

"Is something wrong?" he asked almost condescendingly as he placed his glass on the table.

His tone served only to annoy me further. I could feel my blood boil as I watched him lean forward and pick up the very same baguette Angel had reached for just moments before.

"Hell yeah something's wrong." I hissed through clenched teeth. I didn't need to yell because the power of my words let him know exactly how I felt.

The entire table, which only moments ago was filled with happy chatter, quickly fell silent at my outburst.

"Haaa!" Ethan said loudly, breaking the silence, his shoulders shaking with laughter as he cut into his sirloin.

"Ethan, stop," Monica said, giving him an evil stare across the table.

"I'm not doing anything," Ethan said before taking a bite of his steak. "I knew this was going to happen sooner or later. I didn't just meet this dude yesterday. Pass the steak sauce, please."

"Everything's okay, Greg," Angel said, obviously shaken but still trying her best to diffuse the situation. "Cory, please? Can we just finish dinner?"

"Nah, everything isn't okay," I said, ignoring her while still staring directly at Cory. "This dude has no business talking to you like you're a damn child."

I slid my seat back and stood to my feet. "How about we go outside and talk?" I asked, glaring down at him.

He didn't say anything, instead, his eyes narrowed ever so slightly as he stared back at me.

I slowly nodded my head in affirmative anticipation. I hoped he would. I wished he would.

"Oh my God," I heard Stacey gasp in horror. "Guys, please. Let's not do this. Ethan, do something."

"I am doing something," Ethan responded with a grin as he took a sip of his drink. "I'm going to sit my ass right here and finish my dinner because that's none of my business. This tea though. Delicious!"

I ignored them as I continued glaring down at Cory. I knew exactly who he was, what kind of man he was. I knew he thought that his money gave him carte blanche to treat the people around him with contempt. He was about to learn the hard way that his good job, money, and fancy clothes would be of no use once I got my hands on him. I couldn't hold back the small smile that curled my lips as I thought about the pain I was about to unleash on him.

I know he saw my readiness, almost eagerness to put as much hurt on him as possible. I was taken aback however, because where I was expecting to see fear and intimidation; I was instead met with an expression of boredom. As if to emphasize this, he rolled his eyes before sitting back in his chair, crossing his legs at the knees, and just continuing to silently gaze at me. I knew he was trying to throw me off my game by keeping up his calm, cool, and collected demeanor. Sadly, it was working. I could feel myself becoming even angrier as we continued our silent stare-off.

"Okay? Now what?" he asked, his annoyingly patronizing words slicing through the space between us.

"Shut the hell up," I growled through clenched teeth. "I hope you can swim because if you talk to her like that again, I'll ball your punk ass up and throw you overboard."

I watched as a quick, faint smile spread across his face, gone before I could even register that it was there. He was enjoying this. He was feeding off my rage. I could feel my anger turning into confusion as I continued to stare at him. The longer I looked into his eyes, his hollow empty soulless eyes, I was again hit with the notion that something was off with him.

I shook my head to try and clear my mind, and turned to see the shocked faces of everyone around the table. I could feel the walls of the room closing in around me, and without saying another word, I turned and exited. I needed space. I had to get away from them. I had to get away from him. I needed to get away from her.

13

Celeste

I could hardly contain my excitement as Dante and I made our way through the main dining room. While most of the people in the large, opulent room were seated at tables for four or more people, we had a small table all to ourselves.

"Thank you, baby," I said as I took my seat in the chair Dante pulled out for me.

"No problem, love," he said, as he sat across from me and admired me in a way I had not seen since we first began dating.

"Man...you are looking too good!" he finally said, reaching over and taking my hand. "I know I've said it at least twenty times since we left the room, but damn!"

"Boy, stop," I said with a giggle as I playfully slapped his arm. I was blushing at his comments and loving each and every one of them. It felt so good when he complimented me, and I knew in his heart, he meant every word.

As hard as I worked to keep my body in shape by exercising every day, his appreciation felt good. After working a full shift,

I would go to the gym and put in at least an hour of focused training on my abs, thighs, and butt, trying to keep them as tight and firm as possible. Even with all of that, it saddened me to think that I still hadn't done enough to keep his attention focused solely on me.

"Nah, I can't stop, Celeste," he continued with that huge grin of his. "I mean, damn! I love the way that dress looks on you. You are beautiful."

"Thank you," I said, giving his hand a tight squeeze. I had chosen the fuchsia belted, knit wrap dress because I loved the way it stopped mid-thigh and accentuated my legs. The black, peep-toe high heels not only added to the sexy factor, but complemented the outfit as well. I knew I was definitely looking and more importantly, I was feeling good tonight.

"Thank you for being my wife," he said, his voice taking on a softer, more urgent tone. "I have to pinch myself sometimes. The last two years has flown by and I've loved every minute of them. It amazes me as to how blessed I am to have a woman like you."

"Aw, thank you. And I'm blessed to be with you as well, Dante," I said, my heart bursting with love. The way our vacation had started, I wasn't sure how we would manage four days at sea. Listening to his words of love, I now had a much better feeling about how things would turn out.

"I love you," he said as he held up his water glass. "To many more years of love and happiness."

"To many more," I echoed, raising my glass at his toast. "I love you."

"So, now that we got all that out the way," he said, placing his glass on the table. He rubbed his palms together enthusiastically. "Let's eat!"

"Whatever!" I said, laughing and rolling my eyes at him.

"I'm just saying," he said, pointing to the menu and reading the items listed there. "Listen to this. There's prime rib, grilled chicken breast, flat iron steak, and lobster tails! I don't know which one to choose."

"You can have all of them if you want," I said before taking a sip of my water.

"Huh?" he said, looking up from the menu with a confused expression. "You paid extra for that or something?"

"No, it's part of the cruise," I said. "My director has been on something like ten cruises and he told me all you have to do is ask for what you want. They bring it right out to you."

"Yeah, right. What if I wanted three lobster tails and a steak?" he asked skeptically.

"Then that's what you'd get," I answered matter-of-factly.

"Well, I'll be damned," he said, laughing as he studied the menu items with renewed interest.

As I surveyed him, I thought back to when we met. He was a driver for Sysco Foodservice and delivered to the hospital every week. The hospital was a part of his local route for a year, and it amazed me that our paths never crossed until that day.

I was outside at the rear of the hospital taking a break from the hectic cardiology ward and talking with my co-worker, Alisha. I was venting to her about the stress that the new director of my department was putting me under just as a tractor-trailer rig pulled on to the property. The unit spun around and the huge silver trailer backed up, stopping a few feet away from the dock. The driver—a tall, handsome black man—got out and went to the rear of the trailer to open the back door.

"Whattup, Ali—," he started to say before stopping abruptly when he caught sight of me. He almost walked into the back of the trailer due to the fact that he was staring at me and paying no attention to what he was doing.

I couldn't help but blush as I watched him try to compose himself.

"Damn, Dante," she said with a smile, knocking away the ashes from the end of the cigarillo she was puffing on. "You forget my name or something?"

"Umm...Nah, Alisha. My bad, ma," he said, as he recovered his cool and busied himself opening up the trailer doors, never taking his eyes off me. "I was just distracted. I'll be right back."

He jogged over to his truck, climbed in, and reversed the trailer until it gently bumped against the rubber guards on the dock. After a few minutes, he came over to where Alisha and I were standing.

"Small delivery this week," he said as he handed her the manifest for the cafeteria's order. All the while he was talking to her, he kept his eyes on me.

"Yeah, I see," Alisha said, scanning the list of items on the order before noticing he wasn't paying her any attention.

"I'll go give this to my boss," she said as she inhaled one last drag before flicking away the white plastic tip and heading inside to the kitchen manager's office.

"I'll go with you," I said, following her.

"Hold up. Wait," he said, reaching out to grab her arm. "You aren't going to introduce me to your friend, Alisha?"

She stopped and turned to Dante, looked at me, and then back to Dante. I could see the wheels turning in her head and a sly smile came to her lips.

"Sure. Dante, this is my friend, Celeste. Celeste, this is Dante."

"Very nice to meet you," he said, moving in to take my hand in his, taking full advantage of the opportunity to get next to me.

With him so close, I was able to give him a more thorough once-over. He appeared to be six feet tall and was bald, with dark brown skin. He had wide shoulders and a broad chest, which was accentuated by his uniform shirt. The short sleeves of his light blue shirt had been rolled up almost to his shoulders, revealing a light sheen of sweat on his muscular biceps. I had a weakness for a man with strong, muscular arms and he definitely had a nice pair of guns.

"Nice to meet you as well," I said, enjoying the firm, comforting grip of his large hands.

"Okay, now that y'all are introduced, can I get back to work?" Alisha asked sarcastically as she stepped between us, forcing us to drop each other's hands.

"Whatever, Alisha," I said before turning to follow her inside the building.

I could tell he thought I was going to stay and talk to him. There was no hiding the disappointment on his face as I left him alone on the dock.

The moment the door closed behind me, I leaned back against the wall and exhaled deeply. Dante was truly a handsome man and it took all that I had to keep my composure standing in front of him.

As much as I wanted to stay and talk to him, I knew that would not have been the right play. One thing I had learned over the years was that a man had to hunt. A good man would make the hunt enjoyable, the pursuit pleasurable. A man who knew what he wanted would go about acquiring his desires by using any of the tools at his disposal to make it happen. For some men, they would use money. For others it was their charisma or intelligence. Whatever the case may be, the man must still hunt.

I hope I'm worth the hunt, I thought as I went inside the building. There were several men pursuing me in one way or another. I had gone out on a few dates with one of the interns in the oncology department. While he was an attractive, intelligent man with a promising career, he had the sense of humor of a dead goldfish and the personality of a slab of concrete. There had been a few others since I began working at the hospital, but as I listened to them blather on and on about themselves as we sat in whatever fancy restaurant that they had taken me in the effort to impress me, I knew there had to be something better.

"I'll call you tonight, okay?" I said, sticking my head into the office where Alisha and the cafeteria manager stood going over the delivery manifest.

"Okay, girl. See you later," Alisha said, giving me a distracted little wave.

I went back upstairs and finished my shift, trying my best to keep my thoughts away from my new acquaintance. Later, I was headed out for the day and had gotten into the routine of leaving with one of my coworkers. Ever since another nurse had been attacked in the parking lot a few years ago when she went to her car by herself, we made sure that none of us left the building alone.

As we approached my little red Mini Cooper backed into a parking space a few spots down from her white sedan, I noticed something under my driver's side windshield wiper.

As we got closer, I saw that it was piece of paper folded in half.

"You got a ticket?" she asked.

I removed the paper and gasped in surprise. I couldn't contain the huge smile that spread across my face as I read the carefully handwritten note:

Celeste,

I hope you don't think this is too forward, but I didn't want to search all over the hospital like some kind of stalker. I asked Alisha to tell me which car was yours. The more I think about it, that was kind of a stalker move too. Anyway, I really would like to get to know you better. Please give me a call. I hope to hear from you.

Dante

704-555-6571

I could not hold back the huge grin that spread across my face as I read and reread the handwritten note.

"No, it's not a ticket. It's just something from a new friend," I said to her before hitting the button on the remote to unlock my car.

I called him later that evening and we ended up talking for hours. We did this again the following day and every day after that it seemed. Dante and I quickly grew closer, moving from friendship to exclusively dating. When he proposed to me, it was the happiest day of my life. From that point until now, sitting here together on this cruise celebrating our two year wedding anniversary, I have tried to make sure he was satisfied in every way possible. Seeing where we might be heading, I wondered if maybe I should've tried harder.

I took a sip of my water, quickly pushing away the negative thoughts cluttering my mind. Instead, I surveyed the large dining room, admiring all of the elegantly decked out people seated all around us. I loved to see people dressed up. It was something I rarely experienced, as my attire usually consisted of drab, grey hospital scrubs and clogs worn in a sterile environment of white walls and fluorescent lights.

As I scanned the room, my gaze fell upon the face of a woman I had seen earlier on the Lido deck. She was sitting a few tables away from us with the same group of women, but this time they were all attractively dressed for the evening.

I took in the soft features of her face and was struck by how pretty she was. She was talking to one of her friends, her long eyelashes fluttering as she parted her full, sensual lips to take a dainty bite of a breadstick. Her beautiful, straight, white teeth sinking into the soft bread, mesmerizing me as I watched her.

The woman turned in my direction and our eyes locked for several moments. Her mouth moving slowly as she chewed.

Deliberately, she gave me a small nod and leisurely, seductively ran the tip of her tongue across her lips before turning away. She shifted her attention to a man dressed in blue who passed by her table, her eyes following him as he made his way out of the dining room.

"Okay, I think I know what I want. I'm going to have..." Dante said, breaking me out of my trance. "I'm going to go with the flat iron steak and the Maine lobster tail. Nothing like surf and turf, right? What are you getting?"

"Surf and turf sounds good, baby" I said, attempting to refocus on my husband, trying to stay in the present and resisting the urges that were pulling me back in to my past. "Umm...I think I'll have the grilled chicken breast," I said fumbling with my menu before quickly putting it aside and taking a long drink of water, draining the glass.

Don't even think about it. Don't do it, I thought as I swallowed the cool liquid. I had enough to deal with in the near future and I could not allow myself to let anything, no matter how tempting, distract me.

14

Michal

Kendra and I walked through the main dining room, turning heads once again just as we had earlier on the Lido deck. I ignored the death stares that several jealous women threw in our direction. I knew we were looking good tonight for the first Captain's Dinner, so it was a given that all of the men, including those women's husbands and boyfriends, were gawking at us as we followed the maître d' to our table.

Maria and Regina, sitting at the table waiting on us, each had their make-up flawlessly applied, hair done to perfection, nails immaculate. We were a table full of gorgeous women, and we knew we were the talk of the town, or in this case, the ship. None of the hateful stares that we were getting could stop that.

Maria wore white capri pants with a sheer white top that covered the black bustier underneath. This was as close to dressing up as it came for her as she usually took a more casual approach, preferring instead to wear jeans and T-shirts. As I checked her out now, I was very impressed with her outfit.

Regina sported a sexy, black knee-length dress fitting her figure perfectly. The halter dress with sheer, peek-a-boo sides was not something I ever thought I would see her wear, but I had to admit, she looked great. Her hair, which she usually kept in a simple ponytail, was flowing down in curls over her shoulders.

"Hot damn! Check you out," Maria said. She was gaping in surprise as she marveled at Kendra's outfit. Kendra had transformed the simple pink pantsuit which showcased her newly acquired physique. It was now a more daring ensemble by the fact that she wasn't wearing a top of any kind under the jacket. The cleavage of her bare, brown breasts stood out in contrast to the pale pink outfit, covered only by the jacket's wide lapels.

Kendra's dramatic weight loss had awakened something in her that none of us knew she possessed. Her confidence level had to be off the meter for her to rock such a provocative outfit. And here she was, brashly and fearlessly pulling it off.

"I know, right?" Regina said, agreeing with Maria. "You're doing the damn thing, Kendra."

"Thanks, guys," Kendra said as she sat. "Yes, ever since I lost all that weight, I've been doing a lot of new things. You know, trying to step out of the shell I'd been in for all of those years."

"I hear you," Maria said, reaching over and giving her a high-five. "Keep it up. I'm happy for you, girl."

"Speaking of doing the damn thing," Regina said, turning in my direction. "Michal, girl, you are too fierce in that dress. Just showing off all them legs!"

I couldn't do anything but smile as I thanked her for the compliment. My outfit for the evening was a colorful, sophisticated, thigh-high mini-dress with more than a hint of sexiness.

"Well, ladies," I said after placing my drink order. "It's been so long since we've all gotten together. I know it's not our whole group like usual, but I'm really happy to see each of you."

"Yes, indeed," Maria agreed. "With all the crap I've got going on at home, this trip couldn't have come at a better time."

"Really, Maria?" Kendra asked in a concerned tone. "What's going on?"

"Yes, girl. What the hell is going on with you?" Regina asked in her usual blunt manner. She rarely used the tactful approach, choosing instead to get right to the heart of the subject. "I've been wanting to ask you about you changing your status from 'married' to 'divorced' a few months back. I just never found the right time. So what happened between you and Keith that was so serious that you dropped Tyler and went back to using your maiden name?"

Just as Maria began to speak, our waiter returned to the table to take our dinner orders. After we placed our appetizer and dinner entrée selections with the waiter, we all turned to face Maria, waiting for her to continue.

"Well, trust me, it was serious. In fact, I'm in the process of getting Nyla's last name changed as well," she said after taking a sip of her merlot. "Let's just say that Mr. Tyler, my bastard of an ex-husband, decided he needed more than I could provide him. To be more precise, he needed more than I was equipped to provide."

"Wow!" I exhaled softly, empathizing with my friend's pain, anger and frustration.

"I don't get it though," Kendra said in surprise. "You guys seemed to be perfect for each other. From the minute you met Keith back in school, you two have been inseparable."

"I know," Maria agreed. "I'll never forget when I entered that American government classroom and saw him for the first time. He stopped me after class, asked me out, and things just seemed to fall into place for us."

"Oh my God! I'd forgotten all about that," Regina said. "Damn, you were just starting to kick it with Keith when things got crazy with Darlene and her college sweetheart. Wow! It's crazy how Darlene has always been going through so much, even back then. It doesn't make any sense that any one person should have gone through all of the stuff she had to at such a young age."

We all nodded our heads in agreement. In the midst of the somber silence that settled over our group, I was transported back to our days at Texas Southern. The memories of Owen Knight, the man that Darlene dated when she and I were roommates, came rushing back to me. He loved Darlene and was probably the only person she could open up to and truly trust. The only problem with their perfect college sweetheart romance was that for the majority of the time they were together, Owen and I were having a secret affair.

It is still a mystery as to exactly what happened that night when Owen and a small group of his friends had a confrontation off campus with the Houston police. What we do know is that whatever went down resulted in Owen being shot in the back and eventually dying at the scene. The official report said that the officers feared for their lives when one of the guys pulled out his wallet, even though that was what the officer who shot him had commanded for him to do.

After the incident, there was supposedly a thorough investigation conducted by the department. Despite eyewitness testimony from his friends, all of whom luckily were not hit by the salvo of bullets fired, along with dozens of other witnesses, ultimately neither of the officers faced any charges. Except for them being ordered to take target practice training, there was no real disciplinary action taken within the department for the fact that over twenty-four shots were fired at the unarmed men.

Once the report, which cleared the two officers involved of any wrongdoing was released, Maria, who had always been interested in law enforcement, switched her major from political science to criminal justice. Her ultimate goal was to work in an agency, focusing on internal investigations, in order to make sure that police officers conducted themselves to the highest standards possible and were held accountable when they didn't.

Kendra's voice cut through my thoughts, bringing me back to the present when she said, "Yes, indeed. Darlene went through a lot, all right. What could you expect though? She was being betrayed left and right."

"Betrayed? What are you talking about, Kendra?" Maria asked, looking at her in surprise.

"Nothing, girl. Don't worry about me. This wine just has me a little tipsy," she said, taking another sip of her shiraz to emphasize her point. "Anyway, what were you saying?"

"Well," Maria continued, "It was love at first sight from the first moment I laid eyes on him. Before I knew it, we were graduating, getting married, moving to Austin, starting a family by having Nyla—the whole nine."

"That sounds like a fairytale come true," I said, trying to understand how things went so tragically wrong for them to where their seemingly happy marriage had ended in divorce.

"Yeah, I guess it would from the outside looking in," Maria said wryly. "But like I said, I wasn't equipped to give Keith what he needed. What I mean is that—"

Once again our waiter came back to the table, interrupting us. We again waited patiently as he placed our plates of delicious smelling food in front of us. We bowed our heads as Kendra quickly blessed the meal. She had barely said amen before Regina spoke up, urging Maria to continue.

After taking a bite of her flat iron steak, Maria took a sip of water and continued. "We were both doing well at work. Keith was even coming up on his time to be eligible for a promotion to detective within the Austin Police Department. I was making strides on the force too, so like I said, things were going well. The whole time though, I didn't know what it was but I just had this feeling that something wasn't right. I mean, damn, I'm a cop and a woman, so I know when something just isn't adding up."

We all chuckled at that comment. Maria had always been nosy to begin with and when something caught her interest, there was no way you could shake her off the scent.

"So anyway," she continued, "I did some digging through his cell phone and came across a few text messages that were shocking, to say the least. I couldn't believe what I was reading, but I didn't say anything to him about them. Maybe I was in denial or something, but I refused to let myself believe he would do me like that. So, when Keith told me that he would be on an overnight stakeout with his partner, I decided to follow him. I left Nyla with our next door neighbor and I followed his cheating behind right to a fleabag hotel."

"Oh no!" I gasped, my imagination kicking into overdrive. I could just see Maria trailing her husband to a seedy hotel in a rundown section of town, kicking in the door and catching him and his side chick.

"Oh, yes," she said, the hint of an evil smile coming across her face as if she was reliving that night. "I went into the hotel, flashed my badge to the front desk clerk, and got a key to the room he was in."

"Who was she? Did you know her?" Regina asked excitedly.

"You could say that," Maria said disdainfully. "I entered the room and saw my husband bent over on that nasty hotel bed, face down in the sheets, getting pounded from behind by his partner. Andre. His male partner. His big, muscle-bound, body building, male partner. His partner that had come over to our house to hang out too many times to count."

We all instantly stopped eating, our forks hanging in mid-air, just staring at her with our mouths hanging agape. There was nothing anyone could say as we were all in absolute shock.

"Yep, that's the same reaction I had," she said with a joyless chuckle, her eyes filling with tears as the pain of that moment seemed to return. "My husband. The father of our daughter, was living a lie. He was one of those down-low brothas, and I caught him in the act. I couldn't say anything. All I could do was stand there, watching them, listening to Andre's grunts of exertion mixed with Keith's disgusting moans of pleasure. I got sick to my stomach, turned around, and left as quietly as I had come in. They didn't even know I had been in there. I went back home, packed my stuff, got Nyla, and never looked back."

I didn't know what to say. It seemed as if none of us did. We were absolutely speechless as we processed the story we had just heard.

"I'm just glad I'd left my side-arm at home," she said with a weak smile.

"Aaww, I'm so sorry, girl," Regina said, getting up from her seat and moving around the table to hug her. We all followed

Regina's lead and formed a small circle around Maria, trying to comfort our friend.

After a few minutes, we each returned to our seats, wiping the tears from our eyes, each of us feeling the pain Maria must have experienced. We listened as she quietly told us about how she moved from Austin to Killeen, the city right outside of Fort Hood, one of the country's largest military bases. She had been there for the last six months, having taken a job with the Killeen police department and trying to move on with her life. She had gotten a few phone calls from Keith to let her know he had moved to New Orleans and joined the police department there. He wanted to see Nyla, but up to this point, he hadn't done anything further to try and contact them.

I reflected on Maria's words, focused not so much on what Maria herself had gone through, but trying to imagine what Keith was going through as well, keeping his secret from his wife. I had an idea as to how difficult it was to keep secrets from those closest to me. It was a struggle, day in and day out, to keep your desires under control. However, when you are able to release, to be open, to be free, it was truly a liberating and powerful experience.

"Michal? Earth to Michal, you there?" Regina said as she poked at me with a breadstick. "Can you come back down here with the rest of us?"

I couldn't help but smile at Regina. She was the anchor of our group, always there to bring everyone back up, no matter what we might be going through. "I'm here, girl. I just zoned out for a minute," I said, taking the breadstick from her.

I was still smiling as I surveyed the crowded dining room at the faces of the many people enjoying their meals. I had just taken a bite of the breadstick when I locked eyes with a beautiful woman. She was sitting at a table not too far from us with a handsome man I assumed to be her husband. After listening to Maria talk about Keith and his secrets, I knew it was time for me to act. I only had three more days and nights before the cruise would be over.

I gazed into her eyes and even with the distance between us, I knew she would be one. I didn't know when or where or how, but she would definitely be one. I nodded my head, affirming my decision, just as a tall, muscular man dressed in blue linen strode confidently by the table. I turned from her and focused on him, watching as he left the dining room, admiring the way his brown skin contrasted with the soft color of his ensemble.

He might just be one as well, I speculated before returning my attention to my friends.

15

Greg

The cloudless night sky overhead seemed to stretch as far as the eye could see. I leaned on the railing of the ship, taking in the majestic scene, admiring the thousands of stars shimmering and dancing above.

I took a long sip of my cognac, enjoying the smooth burn of the top shelf libation as I swallowed. I was wrapped up in my thoughts, my feelings, my anger, all centered around Angel.

Never in a million years would I have thought I would find anyone that could capture my attention, both physically and mentally, the way that Angel did. Ever since the chance encounter at a Super Bowl party back in January when I met her, we had been together. From phone calls throughout the day to falling asleep holding each other at night, we were together.

I had fallen in love with her. I never believed something like that could happen between us, but before I knew it, there I was, head over heels in love. It was only a few weeks ago that she and I were together. Somewhat. And now, we weren't.

For the brief few months our relationship had lasted, we chose to keep it as our little secret. We kept it in the dark, hidden from even our closest friends. But it was still a relationship nonetheless and I felt we were moving to a point where we could come forward and tell everyone about us. Those feelings were crushed when she showed up on the arm of her new boyfriend at the restaurant that night. If it wasn't for a case of tragically poor timing on her part, I probably would never have known how she really felt about me—about us. I was operating under the mistaken belief that she and I were building towards something special when obviously, she had other ideas based on the way she abruptly ended things. I thought she wanted a man to treat her like the queen that she was, to be there for her, to love her unconditionally. Instead, it turned out she wanted a man that could provide her with more. More things, more material possessions, more money. But was he providing her with more happiness?

I always knew that sooner or later, something like this would happen. I just hoped when it did, the feelings that had developed between us would allow her to see past the differences between the amounts of our paychecks and bank account balances. I knew when I met her she wasn't some destitute bag lady living beneath an underpass downtown somewhere. Angel was an educated woman, having earned her MBA from Georgia State University. She was a top account manager for one of the largest advertising and marketing firms in Atlanta, and doing quite well for herself. It was no wonder that she wanted a man who matched her financial and social status. It broke my heart every time I thought about the night she told me I couldn't give her the things she desired right now and how she couldn't wait around to see if I would be able to do so later on. She made her decision, chose Cory, and there was nothing I could do about it.

Witnessing her with Cory tonight, I could see she wasn't truly happy. There was no hiding the pain written all over her face. It was clear as day to me. I could see it even if no one else could because I knew her so well. In the time she and I were together, I learned everything about her. I was tuned in to her moods, her likes, her dislikes. I learned how she needed to be treated, how she liked to be pleased. Watching him with her, I knew he wasn't giving her any of the things she really needed.

"I'm glad I finally found you," a sultry female voice behind me said.

Her voice.

"Yeah, just taking some time to myself," I answered, not turning around to look at her. I was sure the darkness around me probably would have prevented it, but I didn't want to risk her seeing the way her presence caused the happy smile on my face and the heartache in my soul.

"Thank you," she said quietly.

"Thank you? For what?" I asked in confusion, draining the last of my drink. My back still to her, I focused on the empty glass, willing myself to keep from turning around and facing her.

"Yes. Thank you for standing up for me. I know he can be a bit forceful at times, but he really is a good guy."

"Forceful? A good guy?" I spat, hurling the empty glass into the distant ocean before spinning around to face her. "Angel, are you serious? He doesn't respect you. If he talks to you like that in public, I can only imagine how he is with you in private. I can't believe you chose that fool over me."

"I know," she said softly. She looked at me with those beautiful, brown eyes that I missed so much. I felt myself getting weak as I took in the soft features of her face, the high cheekbones, the perky nose, the full lips.

We were silent for several minutes, each scrutinizing the other. My eyes moved downward, moving to her delicate shoulders, her full breasts, her firm stomach, her narrow waist, her thick hips, her muscular thighs, her small feet. My heart and my body missed her so much.

Angel's eyes followed mine, watching me watch her. As my gaze made its way back up to her face, our eyes met and locked. Even in the muted light of the stars, I could still see the craving in her eyes, and I knew she saw the fire in mine.

In two quick steps, she was standing in front of me, her body on mine, pressing her soft lips to mine, pulling me into a powerful kiss. Our tongues met, danced with each other, the prelude to passion.

Grabbing her gently around her waist, I pulled her even closer to me, so close I could feel her heart beating wildly against my chest. I moved my hands down, cupping the plump curve of her behind, my fingers tracing over the firm flesh. As I ran my hands across the thin fabric, my mind registered what was not there.

She broke our kiss and stared at me with eyes filled with lust. Reading my thoughts, she looked at me with a sly smile before answering my unasked question, "I'm not wearing any."

Stepping backwards into the shadows formed by the overhang of the deck above, she pulled me towards her. Turning around and placing her back to me, she began to slowly grind her rear end against my fully engorged manhood. This woman knew exactly what buttons to push and was well aware that it was only a matter of time before I lost all control.

Reaching behind her, she deftly unzipped my pants and unsheathed my fully armed weapon which was standing at attention, locked and loaded, ready to commence carnal war.

"Do you miss me, baby?" she whispered over her shoulder, her voice audibly teasing me while her fingers which were firmly wrapped around my member, physically did the same.

"Yes...Yes...Hell yes, I miss you," I moaned, my body growing weak with each magical stroke of her fingers.

I couldn't take it any longer. I put my hand in the small of her back, gently pushing, causing her to bend over at the waist. She obliged without resistance, her dress pulled up and legs spread apart to allow ease of access to all of her.

Placing my organ at the edge of her entrance, I did a quick scan of the empty deck area around us. Satisfied we were still alone and out of sight of anyone that might happen to pass by, I wasted no more time. I pushed deep inside of her, my path met with no friction as she was more than ready for me.

She released a whimper of pleasure at my emphatic entrance into her. Filling her completely, I stopped only because I could go no deeper. I savored the feeling of her body gripping mine before I slowly pulled out of her. I repeated this over and over, each thrust becoming more forceful, more aggressive than the last.

The sound of the ocean waves hitting the ship's hull was barely enough to mask the sound of her muted cries of ecstasy. I tried to pound the pain out of my broken heart with each powerful thrust into her. The hurt, the embarrassment, the disappointment, the rejection, all of the emotions that I had been carrying inside of me since the night she ended things fueled my passionate onslaught.

My pace quickened as I felt that blessed end draw near. I felt it building and then finally, the explosion came. My release was so tremendous that my legs grew weak causing my knees to buckle.

Angel squirmed with pleasure as I released inside of her. She threw her hips against mine, trying to take in all of me, not wanting to lose a drop of the liquid love being injected into her very core.

I took a few minutes to allow my heartbeat to slow and my breathing to return to normal. Pulling out of her, I saw that the midsection of my linen pants were soaked with her essence, the evidence of our passion staining the fine material.

After taking a few moments to compose herself, she pulled down her dress and turned to face me. She had a seductive smile blended with amusement and satisfaction.

"Damn, baby," she said, nodding in approval. "You are truly the best. My God, I missed that."

"So now what?" I asked, glancing over at her as I zipped up my pants.

"Well, now we go back to where we were," she said quietly, her smile fading. "Nothing's changed, Greg. I'm staying with Cory. In fact, I have to go because I know he'll be looking for me. I have to figure out how to get cleaned up and wash your scent off me without him getting suspicious. But don't worry, Ill see you again."

With that, she kissed me on the cheek, turned, and casually sauntered away. I watched her leave me yet again, her exit ripping my heart open anew, allowing all of the pain to flood right back in.

16
Michal

Finally, the coast was clear and I was able to step out of my hiding place without being seen. My body was tingling with excitement from everything I had just witnessed. The energy that seemed to come from the power of their intense interlude was still coursing through me and I knew I had to get back to my room quickly in order to let it out.

Not even thirty minutes ago, my girls and I had just finished with dinner. We were standing outside of the dining room waiting on the elevator and as luck would have it, I was standing only a few yards behind the sexy specimen of a man I had observed earlier.

A little while ago, he had gotten up during dinner and quickly walked out the exit. The instant that I saw him moving through the dining room, I recognized him from earlier on the Lido deck. There was no way I could have avoided seeing him as his height, body, and distinctive outfit drew my eyes to him. I was more than impressed with the way the light fabric of the blue linen outfit fit on his muscular physique. When he passed our table, I had an inclination to follow him to see what I could get started. I decided against that and a few minutes later, he came back into the dining room and stayed with his group for a while longer.

I wasn't sure what to think at first since his group consisted of what seemed to be three couples and two single guys. The more I observed them however, the more confident I became that the two guys were not on the cruise together romantically.

Him returning couldn't have worked out any better for me. After a few moments, they all got up from their table right at the same time that my girls and I were preparing up to leave.

As I stood close to him amongst the mass of people waiting for the elevator, I could tell he was all man. There was something about him that led me to believe that he had the potential to do exactly what I needed to have done.

I stood in the lobby talking to Maria all the while watching him out of the corner of my eye. Suddenly, he said something to his friend before turning to leave.

"Excuse me," he said in a deep, masculine voice as he brushed by me on his way out of the lobby. In that brief moment, I was able to take in the alluring trail of Bulgari cologne he left in his wake.

I watched until he disappeared behind the wall of people in the small space. At that moment, I knew it was time for me to make my move.

"Hey y'all. I'm going to go get some fresh air. I'll catch up with y'all later on, okay?" I said, turning to go in the same direction that he had went. Hopefully I would be able to catch up to him before he got too far away.

"Everything okay?" Regina asked.

"Oh yeah, I'm fine," I answered quickly, using a reassuring tone. I hoped none of them would want to go with me. That would have totally ruined the devious plan I was forming. "I'm not ready to turn in yet. I'm going to walk off that huge dinner before going to bed."

"Mmm hmm," Kendra muttered under her breath.

What's wrong with this woman? I asked myself, cutting my eyes at her, my annoyance growing. She had been making those little sarcastic comments all throughout dinner. I chose to ignore her however because I was now on the hunt, my prey somewhere in front of me on the verge of escaping. I had plans and was not going to let Kendra or anyone else distract me from the task at hand.

I went through the sliding glass door leading outside and there he was. Even through the murky darkness, I was still able to make him out in his blue outfit as he leaned against the ship's railing about fifty feet away. With the amount of people crammed on the ship, I was surprised that except for a few stragglers here and there, the deck was relatively free of any other passengers. I took it as a sign that he was by himself, gazing out into the dark shadows of the water below.

Now's my chance, I thought, my heart pounding with excitement. The adrenaline kicking in as I started moving towards him, I had only taken a few steps in his direction when

I heard the door slide open and then close behind me. I glanced over my shoulder and saw it was one of the women in his group. I stopped and leaned against the railing, allowing her to pass by me. I watched her walk over and engage him in conversation before I quickly darted into my hiding place and out of their view.

While I could not make out anything that was being said, the energy between them was unmistakable. I wasn't sure what was going on but I was intrigued. I decided to stay put and continue to watch them, waiting for her to leave before I made my move.

They talked for a while before she moved in and kissed him. This lasted a few moments and then they stepped away from the railing and into the shadows behind them. I could not believe my eyes, but right then and there, he had her bent over and was going to work on her. I could tell she was trying to hold herself back, however, her muffled screams and moans were still loud enough to be heard over the waves hitting the side of the ship. Her sounds of passion carried through the night air to where I was hiding allowing me to both hear and see their live lust scene play out right in front of me. I was so aroused and it took all the willpower that I had to keep my hands from going south and doing some exploring of their own.

Finally, after a few minutes, they finished, gathered themselves and then the woman left without another look back. The man in blue stayed behind, still standing in the shadows by himself, looking at her as she walked way, almost as if he was hoping that she would come back.

I waited for a little while longer to make sure that did not happen. Confident that she was not returning, I knew that now was the time for me to make my move. I slowly stood from where I had been crouched down behind a stack of folding deck chairs, and went over to where he was standing, my heels clicking on the wooden deck.

"You okay over here?" I asked, the voyeur revealing herself.

"Umm...yeah. I'm good, thanks," he said, obviously startled by my sudden appearance.

"You sure about that?" I asked, giving him my sexiest smile. "I think I have something that could help you with that." I pointed at his crotch and winked at him.

"Huh?" he asked with a look of confusion, subconsciously putting his hands down in an effort to cover the region.

Reaching into my clutch, I pulled out the small tube of fabric stain remover I always carried with me for clothing emergencies. Still focused on his crotch, I licked my lips and remarked, "That's pretty big, don't you think? I'm sure that I can help you with that though."

His eyebrows shot up at the brazenness of my statement. As he silently processed my words, he was also watching me closely, studying my face. Suddenly, a look of recognition flashed over his handsome visage.

Yes, you saw me earlier just as I saw you. You liked what you saw then and I know you are liking it even more standing in front of you now, I thought as a smile of satisfaction spread across my face. I knew I had made the right move and things were falling perfectly into place. My first target was mine to have. Not right now though, but soon enough.

"The stain. That's a pretty big stain on your pants," I said coyly. "I think I can help you get it out with this."

"Ohh!" he said. "Yeah, I must have spilled something on them during dinner."

"Oh, really now?" I asked with a small laugh. "Spilled something, huh? That's funny considering the dance you and your partner were doing a few minutes ago."

"You saw that?" he asked in surprise.

"Yes, I saw all of it. Heard all of it. Loved all of it," I said, staring directly into his eyes.

"No doubt, huh?" he asked with a sly smile.

"No doubt," I repeated. "Now let me help you with that and then we can talk, okay?"

"Help me how? And talk about what?" he asked in a skeptical tone.

"I'll show you," I answered, giving him a quick wink. "I promise I won't bite—that hard."

"Okay, all right." He chuckled. "I guess I'm cool with that."

I gently pushed him against the wall behind him, back into the deep shadows. I pulled the cap off the stain remover stick before dropping down into a squat in front of him. Putting my face eye-level to his treasure, I quickly unzipped his pants and reached my hand into the open fly. With my left hand behind the thin fabric to keep it taut, I place the tip of the applicator pen to the stain and moved it back and forth, allowing the solution to saturate the material.

As I did this, I could feel his manhood grow, straining to break free of his underwear. I teased him with my touch as I did this, my hand brushing against him in soft, tantalizing touches. I was pleased with his size, once again reassured I had made the right choice.

My task concluded, the test completed, I stood upright and stepped back away from him so that he knew I was finished.

"So what now?" he asked in a voice husky with excitement. Having gathered himself, he moved towards me but stopped short, as if waiting on me to make the next move.

"Well, I wasn't able to get it out. It's way too big. We are going to have to go back to your room," I answered flirtatiously before turning and walking away from him. I smiled to myself, satisfied that he was following as evidenced by the sound of his footsteps on the deck behind me.

Soon enough, I thought as I passed through the sliding doors and over to the elevator bank. The lobby was almost empty as we stood in front of the elevator doors and waited for one to stop on our floor.

Standing close behind me, he reached out and put his hands on my hips.

"Don't want anyone to see my...stain," he whispered into my ear, his breath warm on the back of my neck.

"So true," I said, turning my head to respond as I backed up even closer to him. "That would be so embarrassing. We wouldn't want that, right?"

Damn! Definitely the right choice, I thought as I felt his substantial manhood pressing into the small of my back.

The elevator opened and we stepped inside, our bodies so close that I could feel his heat through the thin fabric of our clothing.

We rode the elevator in silence, the muted hum of the blood rushing through my ears the only sounds I heard on the short trip up to his floor.

Getting off the elevator, we walked in step, two soldiers in the army of lust, marching off to do battle with our bodies. A few minutes later we were in front of his room, me facing the door with him right behind me.

"So what now?" he asked, reaching around me and using his keycard to open the door.

"Hold on," I said, reaching and out grabbing the handle to keep the door from opening completely.

"Greg, that you?" A male voice from inside the room asked over the sounds of the television.

"Yeah, dude. It's me," my mystery man answered.

I did a quick pivot which made our bodies turn so now he was standing with his back to the door and me in front, facing him. I gently put my hand on his broad chest and pushed him backwards into the open doorway. "I'll see you again so that you can repay what you owe. Okay, Greg?"

"Cool. You know my name, my room…but I don't know anything about you. What's your name?" he asked, standing there, watching as I turned to leave.

"Desiré," I said over my shoulder as I walked down the hall from his room, giving him the name of my alter-ego, the person I became when I went on the prowl. I usually never asked their names because in truth, I didn't care. I knew that what I wanted from them, needed from them, desired from them, did not require any intimacy. The trivial details such as their names, occupations, the car they drove, the city they lived in, or even their marital status was inconsequential. We didn't need to get to know each other on any level beyond the physical. After I had gotten what I needed, there was no need for any further contact.

I went straight to my room, undressed, got in the shower, braced my foot against the wall and used the warm water from the pulsating shower head to aid me in releasing the energy that had been aching to be freed.

17

Celeste

*O*nce again, the chefs in the ship's kitchen had showed out. After indulging on yet another meal that was beyond delicious, I sat back and rubbed my extra-full belly, feeling exactly like the proverbial stuffed thanksgiving turkey. I started out with just one serving, but my inner fat kid took over, and I ended up ordering a second broiled snapper filet. Just like the first, it was also cooked to absolute delicious perfection.

I was now paying the price for my gluttony, as the meal was sitting on my stomach like a ton of bricks. I was so glad Dante suggested we go for a walk around the ship, because not only would that give my stomach a chance to settle, but it allowed us the opportunity to connect with each other while exploring the ship.

Taking my hand in his, we strolled together and window-shopped all of the various stores selling goods priced lower than

I could believe were possible. Everything from top shelf alcohol to jewelry, cigarettes, perfume, and any other item you could think of.

As we stopped in front of a display of high-end watches, I was suddenly hit with a feeling of intense melancholy. Sadly, for the last several months, this was happening more often than I cared to count. I would fall into a deep funk, becoming withdrawn, and end up snapping at Dante for the smallest thing. I knew the source of my sad mood was due to what he had done. Because of this, I was struggling to handle and process my pain.

We continued walking along in silence with Dante being completely oblivious to my inner turmoil. I tried to shake these negative thoughts out of my head and push the pain from my heart. I wanted so much to just enjoy this trip with my husband and not dwell on all of the mess fermenting back home. I wanted to celebrate our anniversary, but I knew if I let the sadness overtake me, it would ruin what could very well be our last vacation together.

Before long, we ended up at the large theater at the front of the ship. We peeked inside and were pleasantly surprised that there were hardly any people in the spacious auditorium. A quick check of the posted schedule noted the next show would be starting in twenty minutes.

"You want to check it out?" he asked.

I hesitated for a second before finally answering, "Sure, baby. That's fine." My mind was a blur of thoughts, my heart, a hive of rushing emotions as the memory of the reason for my current state of unhappiness filled my consciousness.

I exhaled in an effort to clear my head. We decided on two seats a few rows back from the stage and settled in to wait for the show to begin.

"I'm as full as a tick," Dante said in an obvious attempt to break the awkward silence that had settled between us. He had a goofy grin as he turned to face me and patted his stomach.

"You should be. You damn near ate a whole side of beef," I said, laughing as I reached over and rubbed his usually flat and firm stomach which was now slightly bloated.

"I was following your lead," he said, joining in with my laughter. "I only got another steak because you ordered that second plate, remember? So it's all your fault."

"Oh really? My fault?" I asked sharply, his simple, innocuous statement sparking something inside me, instantly returning me to the dark space I was trying so hard to escape. *Why is everything he does always end up being my fault?* I asked myself, feeling a surge of anger rising in me.

"Well, not your fault. You know what I mean," he said, trying to backpedal from his comment. I could tell he wasn't exactly sure what he had said that caused the change in me. But, whatever it was, I knew he wanted to get away from it as quickly as possible.

We sat in silence for a few minutes, listening to the music of an orchestra playing softly through the theater's sound system. There was so much I wanted to say to him, but I could not find the words to give voice to the sadness inside me.

"Celeste, what's going on?" Dante suddenly asked, turning in his seat to face me directly. "You've been going Jekyll and

Hyde on me for the last few months. I don't get it. One minute we're good, the next you're jumping down my throat."

I thought about his question, my mind churning, my heart pounding. I couldn't bring myself to look at him as it was just too painful. Instead, I stared straight ahead, unable to acknowledge his question.

"I'm really at a loss," he continued, pressing on with his emotionally driven assault on the wall of sadness that had formed between us. "Does all of this have something to do with that Jonathan dude? Can you just talk to me? Let me know what's going on, please!"

Silence once again filled the void between us. His words however, were still echoing loudly in my mind. I was tired of being trapped in my prison of pain, the walls of which were constructed with Dante's lies and deceit. I knew the only escape would be for me to open the doors, open my heart, open my mouth. "Everything was going fine until a few months ago, Dante," I began softly, my words barely above a whisper.

"What happened? You and him started talking again or something?" he asked, his voice rising in a mixture of panic and concern.

I couldn't stop the small smile that came as I took in his reaction. He was so far off base that it was actually pretty funny. If only he knew that it was him, not Jonathan or anyone else, that was the source of the heartache and pain.

"A few months ago, I found out something that broke me down to my core," I continued, ignoring his question and pressing on with my verbal escape plan. "I had to do a lot of things to get where I am in life. What I found out caused me to lose all the confidence in myself that I have worked so hard to build up."

"What did you find out?" he asked in confusion.

"Dante…I…I," I began, stammering as the words that I wanted to say dissolved on my tongue before I could speak them. I turned away, unable to face him any longer. I closed my eyes, took a deep breath to steady myself before attempting to speak again. I was much calmer now, but my words still tumbled out as I opened up to him. "After Jonathan left, I was all alone in Augusta, pregnant, and didn't know my next move. I did know one thing though, there was no way I was going back home to Durham. Not only would I be a college dropout, but I'd be an unwed mother on top of that. I refused to do that, refused to be that, and so, I had to make some tough choices."

I closed my eyes tightly, trying to push away the pain of my decision which haunted me to this day. I hated myself for the cowardly choice that I made. I sacrificed my child's life so that I could have my own and I have regretted that every day since.

I kept my eyes closed, unable to look at Dante for fear of the judgment I was sure would be etched on his face. I knew he was struggling to wrap his head around the latest bombshell from my past I had to drop on him.

"I did what I thought I had to do," I continued quietly, nervously rubbing my hands together as I spoke. "It hurts me so much, but I did it. You can't understand how much that decision hurts me, haunts me really, to this day."

"You're right, I don't think I could ever understand," he said soothingly, reaching over and taking my hands in his. "Like you said though, you did what you had to do."

I opened my eyes and regarded him for a moment and gave his hand a small squeeze. I know he could see the mask of fear and uncertainty covering my face, but even still, his words comforted me. I wiped away the tears and fought to keep my resolve. Not only for my mental health, but for the health of our relationship as well.

"I couldn't stay in Augusta any longer," I said, my voice choking up with the raw emotion caused by my memories. "I had to get out of there, so I reached out to one of my friends living in Atlanta. I moved in with her and started going to school there. Money got really tight, but my pride wouldn't allow me to ask my parents for help. Anyway, that's when I met Tameka, or Tasty, her stage name. She was going to school during the day, and was a dancer at night."

"Oh really?" Dante said with a chuckle. "So she was one of the few dancers actually stripping to pay for school, huh?"

"Yes, she was." I had to smile at that comment. "She was doing her thing, though. Dean's list every semester all the while working until two and three in the morning damn near every night."

"That's pretty impressive," he said, nodding his head in approval.

"Yeah. Anyway, Tameka and I were always hanging out together whenever we didn't have class or neither of us had to work," I continued. "Next thing I knew, she and I were in a relationship. We were together for about eight months before she up and quit the club. She just moved back to her hometown, Jackson, Mississippi, without saying anything. She was the first woman I'd ever been with, and I haven't heard from her since. Once again, I was left heartbroken by someone who I thought loved me. I got over it though. I finished school and moved back to North Carolina. I haven't been with a woman since. Hell, I haven't even wanted to for that matter."

"Do you still like women?" His voice was quiet, he tone eve as he voiced the question that I'm sure was front and center on his mind.

His question transported me to the airport yesterday, my mind replaying the scene in vivid detail. There was something about that TSA agent. I thought I had closed that crazy chapter in my life, but I don't know what it was about her that rekindled those feelings in me.

"I don't know. I have feelings...I have desires. I honestly don't know,." I answered finally, my voice barely above a whisper.

He was quiet for several minutes before he spoke again. "It really doesn't even matter, baby," he said reassuringly. He put his arm around my shoulder and pulled me close to him, saying, "Just know that I love you, and I'm glad you shared all of this with me. I promise never to judge you on anything you've done in your past. We've all done things we don't like and even regret."

I swiveled my head to face him after hearing his last statement. The expression on his face told me that those words were more for him than they were for me. There were things in his recent past I hoped he did in fact regret. His mistakes had directly affected our relationship, having the power to destroy it. I hoped like hell he realized it.

"Thank you, Dante. I love you, too," I said before kissing him on his cheek and laying my head on his shoulder. As we sat together in the theater, I thought about everything I had shared with him. I hoped me finally opening up to him would give him the courage to do the same and tell me his secrets. Would I be able to stay true to my word and still love and accept him if and when he shared his past transgression?

Right as I closed my eyes and prayed for strength and guidance in dealing with everything, the lights in the theater dimmed, signaling the beginning of the performance.

18

Michal

Even after my shower, I could hardly keep still because of the adrenaline buzzing through my body. My erotic encounter with Greg was hopefully just the beginning as it seemed that things were off to a much better start than I could have ever imagined. I hadn't even anticipated making any moves until later on in the cruise, but here I was, like a bad hand in a game of Spades, holding one and two possibles.

Running into Greg was truly a stroke of fortune. I thought finding a single guy like him on the cruise with the necessary requirements would have been almost impossible. It seemed that most men either panicked when they were approached by a bold woman, or they went completely left, becoming way too aggressive. The icing on the cake with him was, from all indications, he was more than physically equipped for the job.

My inner predator had come to life, and I left my room, prowling the ship, thinking, planning, strategizing. I stopped at one of the many bars located throughout the ship, ordered a Cosmopolitan before continuing on. Strolling along, sipping on the drink, which was pleasantly stronger than I had anticipated, I decided to go into the casino and further test my luck.

I walked inside and was greeted by all sorts of electronic noises coming from the many slot machines situated throughout the large, smoky room. Having never been much of a gambler, I preferred instead to makes moves only when I was sure of the outcome working out in my favor. Tonight, however, I didn't see the harm in playing around since I was already here. I made a quick stop at the cashier's cage and got some cash to use for the evening. I only pulled out fifty dollars to play with because I worked too hard for my money and was not about to blow it.

Armed with cash in my pocket and a drink in my hand, I roamed around aimlessly up and down the banks of machines, all vying for my attention before pausing at one of the roulette tables. I was captivated by the wheel which was slowly spinning counter-clockwise, the shifting red and black spaces becoming hypnotizingly mesmerizing. Deciding that I might as well stay and play a few rounds, I took a seat in one of the open chairs.

I studied the electronic display, showing the last 15 winning numbers and their respective colors. There was only an older lady playing at the table. The brightly colored shirt she wore caused her pale, blue-veined skin to seem almost washed out in the overhead lights. I quietly observed her as she methodically placed chips on almost every number on the table.

I finished the last of my drink in a quick swallow, enjoying the slight buzz I felt coming on, and studied the dealer as she gracefully waved her hand in a sweeping motion over the table to indicate no more bets could be placed. My attention went to the small, white ball rapidly spinning clockwise around the outer edge of the slowly turning roulette wheel. I watched in fascination as the ball lost its momentum and slowed before noisily clanking against the wheel, finally settling into the groove for green zero.

It took all of my self-control to not burst out laughing when I saw the expression on the lady's face as she watched the dealer sweep all of her chips away with a swift, practiced flourish. Of all the numbers on which she had placed a chip, the winning number was not one of them. Muttering curses under her breath, the old lady dejectedly got up and shuffled off towards the slot machines.

I took that moment to admire the dealer more closely. She was about five feet, two inches tall with beautiful brown skin, and wore her hair done up in a short, natural Afro. Her uniform shirt and vest were filled out with large, full breasts, and all I could do was nod my head in appreciation.

Another dealer had come over and whispered something in her ear, causing her to produce the most incredibly radiant smile. Our eyes met briefly and she aimed her megawatt smile right at me.

I stopped one of the passing waiters and ordered another Cosmopolitan before taking a seat at the table. I spread out three bills on the soft, green cloth surface, indicating I wanted a stack of red chips.

"Certainly, dear," she said in a sultry voice spiced with a thick West Indian accent.

I looked into her eyes, pausing for a second before speaking. "Thank you...Martina," I said, reading the name tag on her blouse which stated her name and country of residence. I was impressed as I looked at the Jamaican beauty with the Latina name.

Nodding silently, she replaced the bills with fifty red $1 chips, slid them in front of me, and waited for me to place my bet.

I put chips down on a few numbers across the table, leaning over to reach some of the spaces furthest from me. I glanced up to find Martina staring right at me.

I inhaled softly and watched her eyes roam over my body. "May I help you?" I asked at the same moment her eyes moved up and met mine. She averted them when she realized she had been caught staring down the front of the loose-fitting T-shirt that I had put on after my shower. Gathering herself, she silently waved her hand across the table to indicate no more bets could be placed.

I smiled with satisfaction and sipped my drink, waiting for the ball to finish orbiting the wheel. I broke the trance the spinning wheel had me in to once again find she was looking at me. She smiled enticingly, gazing directly into my eyes before returning her attention to the wheel where the ball, which had finally stopped bouncing, was now settled in to the winning slot.

"17-black," she announced.

I jumped out of my seat and started clapping excitedly. Doing a quick calculation, realizing I had won a total of $43 due to me having a chip on the number 17 and another on the corners of numbers 17, 18, 20 and 21.

After collecting my winnings, I put down some more chips before sitting back down. Taking another sip of my drink, I surveyed the large room. As I did so, I noticed there were only ten to fifteen people seated at the various tables and slot machines. "I'm surprised I'm the only one here," I said, turning to face her when she asked me to place my bets.

"You're just a little early," she said. "Everyone has been travelling all day to get to the ship. They're in their cabins trying to recover. Tomorrow night though, this place will be filled."

"That makes sense," I said, leaning back in my chair and frowning in disappointment as I watched my chips get swept off the table.

"And why are you up, beautiful? Can't sleep?" she asked as she stacked the collected chips in a tray in front of her.

"No, I sure couldn't," I answered, smiling at her compliment as I began spreading more chips across the table. "I was with my friends for dinner but just like you said, they were tired and decided to turn in. I had a little more energy, so here I am."

"Full of energy, huh?" she asked with a playful smile. "So you're hoping that energy will help you get lucky?"

"Yes, indeed," I said, staring directly at her. "That's my plan."

Pausing in her task of arranging the chips into neat, even stacks, she raised her head to meet my gaze, once again flashing her beautiful smile.

"Oh, really?" she said in her sexy, melodic accent.

"Yes, really," I said, "With so many other beautiful people on this ship, the odds have to be in my favor, right?"

We were both quiet for a few seconds as if we were trying to read each other's thoughts, each other's intentions.

"I was thinking of eating something when I left here," I said finally, moistening my lips with the tip of my tongue. "Can you suggest something good?"

She slowly nodded her head knowingly and let out a low, nervous laugh before answering. "How about I take you to a private dining room when I get off in about thirty more minutes. You can sample the menu and eat to your heart's content. Would you like that?"

"That sounds excellent," I said, a small shiver of excitement running down my spine. "I'll take my meager winnings and wait for you, okay?"

"That will be fine," she said. "I'll meet you in the lobby outside, Miss...what's your name?"

"Desiré," I said as I collected my remaining chips and got up from the table.

After cashing out, I left the clamor of the casino, moving into the quiet calm of the lobby. Sitting down on a plush chair beside one of the many large windows overlooking the ocean, I stared at the dark seas below. I used that moment to take measure of my emotions. I thought about how I enjoyed the current sensation of my body as it now tingled with anticipation. I loved this feeling, this rush, and appreciated it now since I had so few chances to experience it.

I reflected on what I was doing, what I wanted. My desires. My appetites. I had strong needs, strong urges which I had to keep in check for years at a time, being able to let them surface only in the most controlled circumstances. It was very difficult at times, but after years of self-restraint and discipline, I learned just how to do so. I would go for months, years even, letting my inner desires go dormant until I awakened them at the right time. When that time came, the pleasure I was so desperately seeking to enjoy was immeasurable. Like the cap being removed from a shaken soda bottle, my release was volcanic.

This cruise was my chance to allow my appetites to be fed. I thought about the people I had chosen and wondered if they would be worth it. I have been disappointed before more times than not. I only had one chance with each of these encounters as there would be no second chances, no do-overs.

As the thoughts of desire swirled inside my head, it took a few seconds for me to realize someone was addressing me.

"Desiré," the voice repeated, calling out to me, calling the name of my amorous alter-ego.

"I'm glad you waited for me," Martina said as she approached me, seemingly to barely be able to contain her excitement. "I thought you were like a few others I've ran into before that never followed through."

"No games here," I said, reaching out and gently rubbing her forearm, feeling her soft skin warming at my touch.

"I'm glad to hear that," she said, that intoxicating smile once again spreading across her face. "So, are you still hungry?"

"Starving," I answered softly, licking my full lips for emphasis.

"Excellent. Follow me and I'll let you see what's on the menu," she said, her hips swaying as she strode purposefully in front of me.

We didn't speak to each other as we went into the crew berthing area before finally arriving at her room. After swiping her keycard, she opened the door and stood aside, allowing me to enter into her small living space. I was surprised at how tiny it was compared to my stateroom a few decks above. There was a twin-sized bunk bed, a sink, and a dresser along with personal items all crammed into a space not much larger than the walk-in closet in my bedroom back home.

As if she were reading my mind, she pointed to the bottom bed and said with a grin, "Welcome to my master-suite. Please, make yourself comfortable. I know it's not much but it's my home for the next six months."

"It's fine," I said, ducking my head in order to sit down on the surprisingly soft mattress.

"Okay, good," she said. "I'm going to take a shower and I'll be right back. I won't be long."

"No problem, I'll be here," I said.

As I waited for her to return, I took in my surroundings. I knew that cruise ship workers came from third-world countries all over the globe. They signed six-month long contracts to live and work aboard the ship and the money they earned was sent back home to care for their families. Marveling at her Spartan living quarters, I had nothing but respect for what Martina and all of the other hundreds of workers aboard the ship were doing.

A few minutes later, she reappeared wearing a long, white T-shirt, shorts and slippers on her feet. Without her uniform covering her body, I realized she was even more alluring than I first realized. Her rich brown skin was glowing, the result of the warm water of her shower. The curls of her natural hair still held a few drops of water which sparkled in the overhead fluorescent lights. Her erect nipples were protruding like twin peaks under the thin fabric of the T-shirt, and I could feel my excitement building.

"So, where's your roommate?" I asked, pointing at the empty bed above me. I was in an area of the ship off-limits to passengers and the last thing either of us needed was for someone to stumble in on us.

"She just left to work her shift," she answered, putting away her wet towel and hanging up her uniform in the tiny wardrobe beside the door. "She works in the kitchen and is helping to get breakfast prepared. It works perfect for us because when I'm working, she's here and vice-versa. We always have the room to ourselves."

"I see. That's good to know," I said, now able to relax a bit upon hearing that information. I settled back on the bed, reassured with the knowledge we would not be interrupted. I made myself more comfortable, propping my head up with my elbow so I could watch her. As she moved around the room, putting up her personal items and getting ready for bed, I noticed how graceful she was, her movements lithe, fluid, and sensual.

She must have felt me watching her because she turned and locked eyes with me. That familiar smile bracketed by deep dimples reappearing as she looked at me.

"Come here," I said, patting the bed next to me.

She stopped and clicked off the overhead lights. The darkness was broken only by the pale emissions from the small lamp on the dresser in the corner of the room.

Once she sat on the bed, I gently rubbed her cheek before pulling her face closer to mine and kissing her deeply. Her lips were soft and moist and our kiss intensified with each moment.

Moving my hands downward, I pulled up her shirt and cupped her full breasts. Softly kneading her hardened nipples between my thumb and forefinger, my excitement increased as I heard the moans of pleasure escaping from her.

Moving my other hand even lower, I slid it into her loose fitting shorts and felt the soft mound at the junction of her thighs. Her legs parted, allowing me easier access to her center. As I gently manipulated her moisture, she arched her back with the pleasure coming from each back and forth movement of my fingers.

"May I see the menu now?" I whispered.

"Certainly," she said quietly, staring at me with slightly unfocused eyes.

After pulling off her shorts and tossing them on the floor, she slid her body up on the bed, moving closer to the headboard to give me as much access as possible.

I stood and quickly pulled off my T-shirt. Standing in front of her, I slowly reached behind my back and unfastened my bra, one hook at a time. Her eyes were locked on my body, watching my every move with an expression of sensual hunger. Before tugging off my tight khaki shorts, I reached into the back pocket and pulled out one of the small packages that I carried with me in hopeful anticipation of what was about to occur. I stood there, clad only in a pair of red, lace thong panties, and did a slow twirl to show off my body before slinking out of them.

Climbing back into the bunk, I lay down on her and moved my face down to make it as easy as possible for my full lips to kiss her wet ones. Before doing so, I kissed each of her thighs, closing my eyes, relishing the musky scent of her womanhood as it filled my nostrils.

I reopened my eyes, my mouth watering as I surveyed the delicious looking mound of flesh just inches away from my nose. I paused when I saw the sparkle from a jewel in a piercing there. Seeing that, I knew I couldn't hold out much longer. I moved in, carefully positioning the latex dam of decadence in place before planting a kiss on her most sensitive area. She fiercely arched her back, bucking with pleasure as my tongue explored every crease, every fold, drinking in her essences, lapping up her natural moisture.

I wrapped my arms around her thick, curvy waist and pulled her even closer towards me as if wanting to go into her, become one with her. I enjoyed a meal I had been yearning for but could not have. I had been wanting to hold another woman for so long but I had to fight off the desire to feel the curves, the supple skin, the soft touch that only another woman could provide. No matter how much I wanted to, I couldn't allow my desires to take control of me and ruin my otherwise normal life. Tonight, however, I could let go. Tonight, my appetite could be sated.

I relished this moment, knowing I would not be able to enjoy anything like this for some time in the foreseeable future. I moved my head back from her delicious mound and slid my body up, moving my face so I could press my still wet lips against hers.

She gently moved me off her, indicating with her touch that she wanted me to roll over, our roles switching over. We changed positions within the tight enclosure of her bunk, her now laying on top of me, kissing me softly on my lips before moving downward and kissing my chin. She moved lower, gently kissing my neck, then my breasts, kissing first the left and then the right. Moving lower still, she ran her tongue around my belly button and then descended lower, planting soft kisses on my stomach as she made her slow, teasing journey south. I squirmed with pleasure as her tongue reached its dissolute destination.

I reached down and grabbed both sides of her head in my hands, pushing her face deeper into my treasure. I could feel myself reaching that point of ultimate release as she continued working her oral magic on me. As my body convulsed with pleasure, she held my thighs tightly with her arms to make sure her tongue's target stayed right where she wanted it.

Reaching my climax, my body jerking wildly in the tight confines of the penitentiary of pleasure that was her bunk, I let out a soft scream of sheer ecstasy. This was the feeling that I had been yearning for. Something only a woman could provide and for much too long I had been deprived of experiencing it.

The summit of pleasure reached, we slowly returned to earth, holding each other, her soft skin against mine. She was laying on my chest, her head propped up against my left breast. I looked down at her as she dozed quietly. I thought about the past few hours and how it culminated with this fantastic encounter with a magnificent woman. I closed my eyes and sighed deeply, the reality setting in that I had two more to go before Desiré would have to go back into hibernation.

19

Dante

The bright sun peeking through the tiny slat where the two blackout drapes met became unbearable no matter how far over my head I tried to pull the covers. That solitary ray of light seemed to have all of the sun's power concentrated into that one tiny beam, was shining directly on to my face. I tried to burrow deeper into the covers in order to get a few more precious minutes of sleep, but it was too late. I was wide awake and there was no going back to the blissful pleasure of slumber. That battle was lost. The sun had flexed its muscles and forced me to get out of the comfortable bed.

Being as quiet as possible so as to not wake Celeste who was still knocked out, sleeping peacefully next to me, I carefully threw off the covers and fumbled around for my slides. I went over to the drapes and opened them just enough to be able to peek outside through the clear glass. After several minutes of squinting, my eyes finally adjusted to the bright sunshine and I was able to see we that were docked at the port and the mainland of the Bahamas was just a few hundred yards away.

I glanced back over my shoulder and took this quiet moment to study her. Granted, Celeste had to be the ugliest sleeper ever, but looking at her now as she lay splayed across the bed, mouth slightly open as she sucked on her tongue, she was still so enchanting to me.

No matter how many times I tried to tell her, she would never admit she was anything short of Sleeping Beauty when her head hit the pillow. The sad fact was that she was more like Shrek. To say that she snored was an understatement; that would be the same as saying this massive cruise ship was just a mere boat. Celeste's snoring was akin to Barry White singing inside a freight train spinning around in a tornado passing through CenturyLink Field during a Seattle Seahawks home playoff game.

All of that didn't matter to me because I loved her. I was so torn up inside knowing soon, I would have to do the unthinkable and break her heart. I closed my eyes at the pain I would inevitably cause the one person I loved the most.

The rays of sunlight landed across her body, illuminating her, a spotlight showcasing her shapeliness. As I admired her, I knew there was no question that she was more than enough woman for me. Sadly, I doubted I was enough man for her. It wasn't a matter of satisfying her sexually, because I knew she had no complaints with me in that department. The many times that she had literally tapped out after one of our love making sessions reassured me she was well pleased.

Physical gratification aside, my dilemma was so much deeper than that. I didn't know what she would do after I released the burden weighing me down for the last two years. Would she still love me after I told her everything?

The more I dwelled on my self-induced quandary, the more confined the room became. I needed to go outside and clear my head of the unsettling feeling that the walls were closing in around me. I slid the balcony door open, hoping the demon sitting so heavily on my shoulders would leave me and take flight into the clear Bahamian skies.

I made sure not to open the drapes too wide as to not allow any more sunlight to penetrate into the semi-darkened room. I went outside, shirtless in a pair of Carolina blue nylon basketball shorts. I stood on the balcony in the still morning, inhaling the fresh air. I stared down at the deep blue Caribbean water as it lapped against the ship's hull, causing it to have an almost indiscernible gentle side-to-side rocking motion.

Alone with my thoughts, I leaned on the railing with my father's words echoing in my mind. "A real man has character," he would say as we both lay on our backs on the cold concrete driveway of our family home in Concord and worked on the family car, a 1971 Chevy Bel Air sedan we affectionately called "Squeaky."

My father used those sessions to instill life lessons in me, many of which I still carried to this day. He would stress that a real man had character and does the right thing all of the time, in all situations. He never defined exactly what the 'right thing' was, but he told me I would know right from wrong as each situation presented itself. He told me the right decisions would usually be the hardest ones to make; however, the true test of a man's character was being able to make those tough choices and to stand firm in the consequences of those choices.

I gazed out at the still waters of the harbor, which seemed like glass with the bright early morning sun reflecting off its surface. I remembered those few minutes of illicit pleasure two years ago that were the absolute complete opposite of the right thing to do. I had made an incredibly wrong decision; a decision I'll have to live with for the rest of my life.

I unconsciously toyed with the platinum and gold band on my left hand. The symbol of our vows. The symbol of trust. The symbol of unity. I pulled my wedding band off my finger and held it up, feeling as emotionally hollow inside as its center.

Slipping the ring back on to my finger, I continued to play with it, spinning it around as I tried my best to push the past out of my head. That was an exercise in futility as there was no forgetting her and what we did.

I closed my eyes and I could see her face, her features unforgettable. I saw the soft visage of the woman that came into my life at the wrong time. In the blink of an eye, in the heat of the moment, I lost all self-control and now, she and I were permanently bonded.

I shook my head at the painful memory of our meeting almost a month before my wedding. I was trying to earn as much money as possible, working extra days to get whatever overtime I could to make sure Celeste and I started our marriage off with money in the bank. After working my usual Monday through Friday schedule, I would go in on weekends and make any spot deliveries that came up and needed to be covered.

On one particular Saturday, a restaurant in Gastonia was the first of two drops I had been assigned for the day. When I pulled into the parking lot to make the delivery, I was focused solely on doing my job, finishing these two runs, and getting the day over with so I could get home and enjoy the rest of my day. All of that changed, however, as soon as she answered the back door and our eyes met. In that moment, the instant attraction we had towards each other was unmistakable. I don't know if it was the fact that Celeste and I had stopped having sex for the ninety days leading up to the wedding. She was following the crazy suggestion that she had read in one of the many wedding magazines that she seemed to always have her nose buried in those last few months. It could have been the weakness caused by having over sixty days of backed up pressure aching to be released that led to my lack of judgment. Maybe it was the deep bronze color of her skin. Maybe it was the high cheekbones above some of the deepest dimples I had ever seen. Could it have been her intense brown eyes that seemed to see right into me? It had to be the fact that she just radiated sex in a such a primal way that I had never experienced before.

I was speechless as I checked her out from head to toe. Her hair was set in frizzy, shoulder length, light-brown curls, giving her an almost wild appearance. She was wearing a low-cut, tight-fitting T-shirt adorned with the words 'Open 24 Hours' which unabashedly showcased her cleavage. The black leggings that she wore accentuated her narrow waist, which led down to wide hips and a pair of long, sexy legs.

She looked at me, an almost sneaky smile on her face as if she could hear the blood rushing from my brain and flowing south.

When I had finally composed myself enough to speak, I stumbled through a quick introduction, letting her know that I was there with her delivery. She wordlessly stepped back and propped the door open for me. As she turned and sashayed back into the restaurant, I took that moment to appreciate her other blessings as she moved away from me.

The next thirty minutes flew by as I shifted back into work mode. I stayed focused, making the many trips back and forth from the trailer and into the restaurant with my hand truck filled with her grocery items.

Except for the bit of excitement when I first saw her, the remainder of my time there passed uneventfully. When I finished unloading, she came out, checked her order, signed the invoice, and went back into her office. She barely spoke to me, but the energy between us was still undeniable. I was literally sweating when I climbed back into the cab of the truck, not only from the exertion of working, but also from the intensity of our encounter.

The following Saturday, I went in to work and sure enough, I was once again assigned to deliver to her restaurant. The same thing occurred as I pushed the buzzer to the back door. Once again she answered, this time wearing a bright yellow halter-top and a blue, knee length skirt.

I went through my normal routine, rolling the refrigerated products into the walk-in cooler, then taking dry goods into the large pantry. As I brought in the last items of her order, I turned to see her standing in the doorway. The moment of truth had arrived and I knew what was up the minute I looked into her eyes.

Ebonie Wilson came up and put her arms around me, softly, simply, whispering, "I want you," in my ear. Her voice was husky, deep yet feminine, and there was no mistaking she knew exactly what she was doing.

She stepped back and pushed the pantry door closed behind her. From that point on, no other words were exchanged as we fed our bodies the pleasure that we had been craving the first moment we laid eyes on each other. Our act was one born of pure physical attraction, nothing more, nothing less. No love offered. No romance given. No protection used.

That day was the last time I saw her. I got back in the truck and drove away, leaving her restaurant, leaving her. My wedding was two weeks later and followed by our honeymoon.

I was enjoying my life as a happy newlywed until the day my supervisor called me into his office. He wordlessly pointed to his phone before turning and leaving the room, closing the door behind him.

Almost eight months had passed since my one-time encounter with Ebonie. After I picked up the receiver and listened to her tell me about the result of our erotic episode, silent tears began to flow. She delivered the news in a quiet, dispassionate tone and I realized at that moment, my world as I knew it, would soon come crashing down around me.

I didn't know what prompted her to call me after so much time had passed. Whatever her reasons, my state of happiness was forever destroyed as she told me about the positive pregnancy test. I still held out hope that there was a chance that things would work out in my favor. I prayed I would be able to do backflips of joy like the guys on the notorious daytime talk show who had been given a pardon from unwanted paternity when the host read the DNA test results and emphatically declared that they were not the father.

I didn't have that kind of luck. I met with her a few weeks after the baby was born, took the test and sure enough, baby Imani Jayde was my daughter. I could hardly breathe the moment I laid eyes on the beautiful little girl in front of me, looking just like me. From that point, the test was nothing more than a formality to confirm the reality of what I already knew to be true.

Later, as we sat outside of the doctor's office, from the corner of my eye, I saw Ebonie silently take inventory of the wedding band on my finger. The symbol of exclusivity that wasn't there when we met. I didn't have to explain my new situation to her.

She turned away from me at that moment and has never looked back. She has never called me. She has never texted me. She didn't want me to be a part of her life then or my daughter's life now. I have tried countless times to reach out to her, albeit without Celeste's knowledge, but each time Ebonie never responded.

We left the doctor's office that day, each going our separate ways. Ebonie never asked, but I still knew I had to take care of my responsibilities. I opened up a bank account and funded it weekly in order to make child support payments, which I mailed to her restaurant. I hated going behind my new wife's back and making these secret moves, but what else could I do?

I have a woman who I loved with all my heart regardless of my actions with Ebonie that spoke to the contrary. I have a wife that I still did not know how to open up to and tell my gravest secret. How can I come clean to her about my transgression? How can I tell her? I know that my day of reckoning will come soon enough, but I just don't know how to bring myself to devastate her.

The loud sputtering diesel engine of a fishing boat passing on the water below snapped me out of my reverie and back to the present. I stared out at the horizon, watching the sun climbing higher, seeing the sky getting even brighter, feeling the temperature getting warmer. I heard the muffled sound of a voice over the ship's intercom system as the cruise director made his morning announcement about all of the exciting activities planned for the day. I tuned out the man's incredibly chipper voice; it was way too early for anyone to have that much energy and my mind was too distracted to concentrate on anything he was saying anyway.

A pair of delicate hands slid around me as I felt my wife's soft breasts press into me moments before she laid her head across my bare back.

"Good morning, baby," she purred sweetly, pulling me out of my sad past and into her happy present.

"G'morning, love," I answered, not turning around right away so that she wouldn't see the pain in my eyes. *The time isn't right for me to tell her. It will be soon, but not now. Not today,* I thought to myself before finally turning around to face her, pulling her to me and holding her in a tight embrace, never wanting to let her go.

20

Greg

I lay in my bed in the dimly lit room, staring up at the ceiling, my mind still reeling from all of the excitement from the prior evening. From the tense stand-off with Cory, to my incredible rendezvous with Angel, and ending with my intense introduction to Desiré, last night was like a scene out of a movie.

I cleared those thoughts out of my head and went to the bathroom to conduct my morning rituals. Just as I put my toothbrush in my mouth, I heard the room phone ringing. I thought that Evan would get it, but after the fourth ring, I realized that was not going to happen. I quickly spit out the toothpaste and raced to the phone and answered it.

I continued brushing my teeth as I listened to Ethan telling me we would be meeting up on the Lido deck for breakfast to discuss what we would be doing for the day. Just before I hung up, I glanced over at Evan who was still fast asleep in his bed.

He was burrowed so deep under the covers, I wondered how he had managed not to suffocate himself in the middle of the night. As soon as I put the receiver back on the handset, almost on cue, Evan issued a loud snore, confirming he was still amongst the living.

I smiled to myself as a deliciously evil thought entered my mind. Following through on it, I pulled opened the curtains as wide as possible before ripping the covers off him, ensuring that he fully enjoyed the extremely bright sunlight now flooding the room. I smiled happily to myself as I darted back into the bathroom, nimbly avoiding a pillow that whizzed by my ear. I locked the door behind me, my laughter drowning out the curses he was hurling at me.

After getting dressed, a much calmer Evan and I met up with the rest of the group where we decided to spend the day jet skiing. Sitting through breakfast, Angel and I made sure we avoided eye contact.

With our stomachs filled with eggs, bacon, and other breakfast fare, we disembarked the ship. I had gotten so used to moving around, walking and balancing myself against the ship's constant gentle rolling and pitching that I almost stumbled when I stepped on to the large concrete pier. We had only been on the ship for a day, but it was still a strange sensation to be on solid ground.

We quickly regained our land legs as we visited the tourist traps that lined the beach. Afterwards, we checked out a few boat rental vendors, finally settling on one claiming to have the fastest jet skis on the island. This was exactly what we had been searching for as Ethan, Evan, and I were all speed junkies; we couldn't wait to get out on the water to see just how fast these babies would go.

We ended up getting five jet skis—the couples were paired up on theirs—while Evan, Stacey, and I rode solo. As much as he wanted to go out with us, Walter remained on the beach due to his injuries. He didn't want Stacey to have her fun interrupted and it took several minutes for him to convince her to go out by herself. Finally, she relented, gave him a kiss before mounting her watercraft and gently throttled over to where we all idled waiting on her.

Once we left the shallow water of the beach, the waves provided an exciting arena for the kids in us to come out and play. Ethan, being the ultimate competitor, challenged me to a few races. Monica, riding shotgun with him, was hanging on for dear life at times when he would hit a wave that sent their jet ski airborne. She was a trooper though, showing why she was such a good match for him. They switched positions a few times, with her taking over the controls while he held on behind her.

We spent the better part of the afternoon racing each other and jumping waves with reckless abandon. All too soon, however, the time came for us to return to shore. We made our way back in a loosely formed pack, Ethan and Monica leading the way, followed by Corey with Angel seated behind him, then me, Stacey, and Evan following them.

As I studied Corey and Angel cruising about fifteen feet in front of me, I was having a difficult time at making sure I caught the waves at the right angles to avoid capsizing as I kept getting distracted by Angel's bikini-clad rear end bouncing along directly in my line of sight.

Transfixed by her sexy, brown bottom covered only by the skimpy white bathing suit, barely covering her toned body, I realized just how much I missed her. I didn't just miss her physically, but also her fun, energetic spirit as well. I was also struck with another emotion. Recalling our encounter last night, I felt that familiar feeling of anger swell as I thought about her selfishness. As usual, she had gotten what she wanted, but this time, she left me and ran off to go back to him without giving my feelings any consideration.

The more I focused on her, I could feel my anger receding, my emotions shifting instead to jealousy. I observed them together, her close to him, the only thing between them being the thin fabric of her bikini; I couldn't help but be envious of him. Her body may have been next to his now, but I knew in my heart she should be next to me, beside me, with me. It was truly driving me insane thinking about how messed up this situation was.

I missed her. I was angry with her. I wanted her. All at the same time. Being with her last night for those brief stolen moments, only made me want more.

Unable to contain my frustration of watching her hold him, her arms wrapped around his torso, her body pressed close to his bare back, I gunned the throttle, shooting past them. I blew past everyone, leaving them all in my wake, not slowing down until I reached the beach.

After I turned in my watercraft, I went over to a grove of coconut trees to sit and wait for the rest of the group. In the cool shade provided by the large fronds of the trees, I watched as Cory slowly maneuvered his jet ski into the shallow dock area, allowing Angel to gracefully dismount. Once again, the feelings of sadness, anger, and jealousy washed over me.

I had been staring at her so intently that it took a second for me to realize I was now the one being watched. My attention shifted and locked in on the eyes that were focused on me. Cory was looking directly at me, a satisfied smirk playing on his lips. The sickening smile on his face indicating he had read everything written on mine. My expression translated the words my heart was speaking when it came to Angel even though I tried to hide it. It was there for all to see.

I focused on him, but couldn't get a read on what he was thinking or what his next move would be. He parked the jet ski, turned to her, said something in her ear before he turned and walked in my direction. I saw the expression of fear and apprehension that spread across her face as her eyes shifted from him to me.

I got to my feet and took in Cory walking towards me, his strides confident, his approach unhurried, his body surprisingly muscular now that he didn't have on one of the ridiculous outfits he normally wore. As I measured his approach, I thought about one of the most important lessons I learned from my stint in prison—never underestimate anyone. The minute you did, you would find yourself face down on the dirty tiles, bloodied and beaten. Depending on your foe, you might even end up in the infirmary or worse, waiting on your next of kin to be notified as your body lay covered with a dingy white sheet that still bore the blood stains of the last guy who had underestimated his adversary.

I was no stranger to conflict, having been in fights for one reason or another for as long as I could remember. The harsh training of my youth was reinforced by the hard knocks that came with being locked up. During my incarceration, being able to fight and defend yourself was an absolute life or death necessity. The predators that roamed behind those concrete walls hunted the weak, sought out prey, and moved in for the kill the minute that weakness was sensed or timidity displayed. Almost from day one, I had shown that I didn't fall into that category. Several altercations later, I had made it clear that I wasn't one to be messed with.

Before we had even left Atlanta, I told myself I would stay clear of Cory. The dude bothered me, and he knew that I had no love for him. I wanted to make sure there would be no drama over the course of the weekend. As he approached me now, I knew all it would take was the wrong word from him to spark the right kind of ass whooping I had been wanting to give him.

He stopped in front of me, coolly looking directly into my eyes, saying nothing as we stood toe-to-toe. I was braced for whatever he might throw my way. I was relaxed, feet apart, ready to punch, block, and counterpunch. My body was ready, the adrenaline flowing, but it was my heart that was not prepared for the ferocity of his verbal attack.

"It took me a minute to piece things together," he said, his voice low but steady. "I don't know what it is you think you might have, because quite frankly, you aren't her type. Regardless, your history with her is just that...history."

His words hit harder than any punch he could have landed. I felt myself reeling mentality and I tried to counter.

"Look man, I don—" I began but he abruptly cut me off, not giving me the chance to speak or the respect of listening.

"No, you look!" he growled, his voice tone measured but unmistakably aggressive. I looked into his eyes and was taken aback by how empty, how hollow, how devoid of life they were. I had seen that expression in prison too many times to count. *Who was this guy?* I thought, momentarily confused as I recalled similar eyes belonging to men who had been locked away for doing some of the most heinous things imaginable.

"I don't know you and don't want to," he continued. "I don't know what you and Angel had and frankly, I really don't give a damn. You tested me at dinner last night; that will never happen again. One warning: stay away from her, stay away from me, stay away from us. Keep whatever you're feeling on your side of the ship. I'm not going to say it again."

Having finished, he turned and strode away, heading further up the beach to the line of vendors that had set up their shops.

I stared at his retreating back, trying to process what I had just experienced. I then turned to Angel, the center of this storm, his present, my past, who had run up to me, her face full of concern. "What did you say to him?" she asked breathlessly. "Did you tell him about us? Please tell me you didn't mess this up for me."

I shook my head in disbelief at her question. She was only worried about herself. Her only priority in that moment was making sure he didn't leave her. I couldn't bring myself to speak to her, but the expression on my face must have answered her question. She quickly averted her eyes from mine, shifting them down to her feet, before awkwardly shuffling past me to chase after him.

"What was that about?" Evan asked, his voice filled with concern as he and Ethan came rushing over to stand beside me. "You straight, man?"

"Yeah, I'm good. It was nothing," I muttered, trying to control the anger coursing through me. I brushed past them and jogged up the road to catch the waiting shuttle to take us back to the ship.

I pulled my sunglasses over my eyes, using the mirrored lenses to hide the anger and embarrassment evident in them. I wanted this day to be over, this whole cruise to be over. For now, I couldn't wait to get back to the ship so I could have a couple of drinks, calm down, and figure out how to spend the next two days without having to bump into Cory again. More importantly, I had to make sure to avoid any more chance meetings with her.

21

Michal

I sat on my bed, listening to the sound of the running water as Kendra took her shower. My mind was rambling as usual, thinking of everything, focused on nothing. I hated when I got into these moods where it seemed that nothing could calm my nerves.

I thought about things back home, specifically the people there. Just as swiftly as those thoughts entered my mind, I quickly tuned them out. I stopped that train of thought right in its tracks because I knew if I focused too heavily on what was happening there, my resolve might weaken, and I would not be able to finish what I started here.

The shower suddenly stopped and a few moments later, Kendra emerged, a thick white towel wrapped around her body.

"Aren't you going to get dressed for dinner?" she asked, pausing as she opened the closet to give me a quizzical look. I hadn't made a move to change clothes and was still wearing the navy blue capri pants, loose fitting white T-shirt, and Nike running shoes I had worn on our shore excursion earlier in the day.

"Yes, I'm going to get dressed now," I said, my words belied by my lack of action. "I'm just worn out from today, that's all."

"I know, right?" she said as she busied herself getting her outfit ready for the evening. "And it's not like you got a lot of sleep last night."

At this comment, I whipped my head around to face her. She had her back to me, not paying me any attention as she continued getting dressed. I watched as she dropped the towel that had been covering her and slithered her much slimmer figure into a form fitting, light pink romper style jumpsuit, the top of which fit across her chest and strategically covered her bare breasts. Once again, I had to say that Kendra was dressed to kill.

"I guess I need to get my behind up and get dressed," I said, trying to push her comment out of my mind. "Lord knows I didn't come here to stay cooped up in this room."

"I'm sure you'll find someone...I mean something to do," she said with the tiniest hint of a smirk on her face as she stood in front of the mirror applying pink lipstick, the splash of color seeming to pop in contrast to her brown skin.

"Huh? What the hell's that supposed to mean?" I asked, stopping in my tracks and turning to face her directly.

"Nothing, girl. Nothing at all," she said, pressing her lips together making sure her lipstick spread evenly. "Anyway, I'm heading to the dining room. I guess we'll see you later. Maybe."

With that, she picked up the small, pink clutch off her bed and quickly exited, leaving me alone, standing dumbfounded in the middle of the room.

I tried to minimize the impact of Kendra's words, but the truth of the matter was, she was right. I had other ideas for what I wanted to do. I just hoped things would play out the way I anticipated.

I leaned against the closet door for a few minutes while I formulated my plan for the evening. I went to the phone and dialed the number scrawled on a napkin, hoping he picked up. If he wasn't there, then I regrettably would have to call his part of my trip a failure unless I happened to run into him again. Fortunately, there was a good chance of that since we seemed to share nightly dinner reservations in the same dining room. But if not, there was no plan B. Either I got him or I didn't. Win or lose. There was no draw in this game.

I held the phone to my ear.

Ring.

Ring.

Ring.

Ring.

I was just about to hang up when someone answered.

"Hello?" a male voice asked.

The voice was different from his, a few octaves higher, an even tenor compared to Greg's smooth baritone.

Did I call the right room? I thought, second guessing myself.

"Yes. Is Greg available?" I asked, pushing ahead, glad I had gotten his name. I wasn't sure what I would have done if I hadn't.

"Yeah, hold on," he said before the phone rattled as he put it down and called for Greg.

I said a silent 'thank you' in triumph as he confirmed I had the right room. I crossed my fingers in hopes that everything else would fall into place.

"Hello?" The familiar voice said. Relieved, I sat down on the edge of the bed to talk to him and see how things would play out.

"Hi, Greg," I said, hoping he would recognize my voice without me having to identify myself.

A few seconds went by, the few moments of dead air over the connection allowing doubt to creep in. Finally, he spoke, his voice a low purr as he said, "I was hoping I would hear from you again. Desiré, right?"

"Yes, that's right. What are you doing tonight?" I asked, relieved things were moving along.

"Well, we were getting ready to head out to dinner. Why?"

"You feel like skipping dinner and doing something a little more fun instead?"

"Fun, huh? What did you have in mind?"

"I can show you better than I can tell you."

"Oh really. Show and prove then."

"I'll be there in an hour," I said before hanging up the phone. I rubbed my hands together in excited anticipation of what was in store. Things were starting to shape up just the way I hoped they would.

I glanced at the time displayed on the desk clock before getting up to begin getting prepared for the evening. I took a quick shower, then got dressed in a denim mini skirt and black spaghetti strap T-shirt. I checked my make-up before slipping into a pair of sandals and heading out the door.

I went to the elevators, pushed the button that would take me to his room's floor. As I waited in front of the shiny silver doors, I checked out my reflection and smiled, loving what I saw looking back at me. I was sure some people would frown upon what I was doing, but it was really no one's concern but my own. Right? Wasn't it?

Before I could ponder upon this any further, the elevator opened in front of me and I stepped inside, leaving all thoughts of right or wrong in the lobby behind the closed elevator doors.

A few minutes later, I was standing at Greg's door, the moment of truth at hand. I took a deep breath before gently knocking.

The door opened immediately and there he stood, looking even better than he did last night. The pale overhead light in the room reflected off the dark brown skin of his shiny, bald head and showcased his handsome features. His lips seemed almost edible between the precise lines of his neatly trimmed mustache and beard. Wearing a pale blue V-neck T-shirt, white linen shorts, and brown sandals, he was dressed comfortably to go out for the evening. He would soon find out that I had other plans and they didn't involve us leaving the room.

"Hello again, Desiré," he said, taking a step back to admire me. I could tell from the expression on his face that he genuinely liked what he saw.

"You're looking good," I said. "Going somewhere?"

"I really didn't know what you had in mind for the night so I just threw this on."

"So, are you going to let me in? You are alone in there, right?"

"Umm...yeah. I'm alone," he said, completely caught off guard by my questions.

I moved past him and pointed to the two beds. "Which one is yours?" I asked.

He gave a silent nod of his head in the direction of the bed closest to the door. I kicked off my sandals before going over and getting on the bed, leaning back against the soft covers. I stared directly at him as I sat there, my movements causing my short skirt to ride up my thighs, allowing him to see everything that lay beneath.

"I think you are a little overdressed for what I have in mind for tonight," I said, gazing directly into his eyes.

"I see," he said, a noticeable bulge slowly taking shape under the thin linen of his shorts.

He wasted no time in crossing the room and getting on top of me, laying between my open thighs. I kissed his lips, hungry to taste them the minute he'd opened the door.

His body pressed hard against mine, the passion between us was ignited as our tongues hungrily explored each other. He stopped and lifted up on his forearms, gazing down at me, his chest heaving with excitement. I didn't know what was going through his mind at this moment, but I knew exactly what was on mine.

I reached between his muscular thighs and slowly rubbed his manhood through the light material of his shorts. He was everything I remembered him being. I was once again impressed with both his length and girth. His body shivered at my touch, his reaction turning me on even more.

I took further control, rolling him onto his back so that I sat on him with my legs on either side of his thighs just above his knees. I reached down to get what I had been waiting on from the moment I laid eyes on him. I unzipped his shorts and reached into the open fly, deftly maneuvering my fingers through the narrow opening in the cotton layer underneath and pulling out his treasure. Holding him in my hand, seeing it up close, I was even more impressed. I reached over to my purse laying on the bed beside me, opened it, and pulled out one of the gold foil packages from inside. Ripping it open, I pulled out the contents and placed it on the tip of his manhood. I unrolled it, working it down to the base, sheathing his formidable weapon in latex. These exercises in eroticism were not without caution. I knew I played a dangerous game whenever I went out on the prowl for my pleasure pursuits. As I had done the night before, I made sure to lessen my exposure to all of the many potentially negative things that came with my illicit activities as much as possible.

Life shield in place, I leaned forward, ignoring the unpleasant taste of the plastic protection and took him in my mouth. The pressure of my lips, the flicking of my tongue, the force of the suction along with the back and forth twisting motion of my hands as they gripped his shaft caused him to moan loudly with pleasure. I loved doing this because it was one of the few times where I was in complete control. I had him literally in the palm of my hands, and each flick, lick, twist, suck, and slurp could bring him to his knees if I so desired.

As if reading my mind, he reasserted himself, wresting control of the situation, gently pushing me off him before backing away. I smiled as I watched him attempt to recover from the oral onslaught that I had just hit him with.

"Damn!" he said as he gazed at me with mixture of awe and excitement. "You're the real deal, huh?"

"Well, I did tell you that I could show you better than I could tell you, didn't I?" I responded, smiling as I licked my lips.

Nodding his head in appreciation, he pulled his shirt over his head, revealing a well-defined chest. I sat back on the bed, admiring the view as he took off his shorts and tossed them on the couch beside the bed.

"You taking those off, too?" I asked, pointing at the pair of tight, navy blue boxer briefs through which his erect manhood aggressively protruded, demanding attention.

"I might as well, right?" he said with a big grin. "Not really much left to cover up, huh?"

"I'm surprised you could cover all of that in the first place," I said with a wink before getting up off the bed. I quickly unzipped my skirt, allowing it to fall off my waist before stepping out of the garment that now lay pooled around my feet. I then pulled the T-shirt over my head and stood before him, confidently, dressed only in the skin I was blessed with.

He nodded his head in slow approval as he took in every inch of my naked body before slipping his underwear off his hips.

Both of us stood naked, facing each other like two prize fighters before the first bell, the heat in the room rising. Without a word, he made the first move, coming over and quickly lifting me off my feet, my legs instinctively wrapping around his muscular torso.

Greg carried me over to the bed and laid me gently on my back, positioned himself at my opening, and without another word, plunged inside. I closed my eyes, enjoying the overwhelming pleasure his entry brought me, the exquisite feeling of being filled to my core making my entire body quiver.

He proved to be the perfect choice as he gave me all the pleasure my body needed. For an intense eternity that spanned a mere hour, he did everything to my body, in every way, in every position I had been yearning for. He took me to the pinnacle more times than I could count before he reached his own magical release.

As we lay in his bed, the aroma of lust in the room surrounding us like a heavy fog, we were silent, each in our own world. I smiled as I thought about how things were going for me. Two down. I was beyond elated at how this cruise was turning out to be even better than I could have ever imagined.

As my body returned to earth from the heights he had sent it to, I knew I had to leave. "Well, Greg, that was truly fun," I said as I rolled out of bed and reached for my pile of clothes on the floor.

"But you have to go, right?" he said with the smallest trace of amusement as he verbalized what we both knew and understood.

"You know it," I said, zipping my skirt. "All good things must come to an end, right?"

"No doubt. And that damn sure was good," he agreed, getting up and putting on his shorts. "I get it though. What happens on the cruise, stays on the cruise."

I regarded him in appreciation, nodding in agreement. There was no need for awkward goodbyes because he understood what we had done was a one-time thing. I knew I didn't have to worry about him stalking me around the ship. I was reassured in that even if he were to see me again, he knew the game well enough to keep things moving and not make a scene.

Fully dressed, I stopped at the mirror to do a quick check of my hair and clothing. Satisfied everything was in order, I opened the door to make my exit and almost collided with the person standing on the other side. I quickly recognized her as being the woman he had been with on the deck last night. She was wearing a simple black dress, her outfit indicating that she was either going to or coming from the dining room.

Her mouth dropped open as she stared at me, and then past me at Greg. She then took in his state of undress, and turned back to me. Quickly sizing up the situation, an idea popped into my mind and I made my move.

I looked at her to make sure I had her attention before turning around and stepping in close to Greg. I pulled his face down to mine and engaged him with a long, deep kiss.

"Good night, Greg. See you later," I said as I rubbed his chest and looked into his eyes.

Not missing a beat, he said in the most seductive tone, "Good night, Desiré," he said quietly, the sparkle of amusement evident as he smoothly played along.

Glancing over at the other woman, he nonchalantly said, "Hey, Angel," before closing his room door in her face with a quiet but firm thud. It might as well have been a solid door slam for the statement it made.

"Excuse me," I said, stepping around her, stifling a laugh. I knew that not only did we make things messy inside his room, but based on the expression on her face, I had succeeded in being a little bit messy on the outside as well. *Yes, indeed. This trip is definitely turning out to be one to remember,* I thought as I headed down the hallway away from his room.

22

Celeste

I drained the last few ounces of my mojito and was nibbling on a tart piece of lime pulp, reflecting on just how good today turned out to be. Sitting with Dante in a cozy booth at the back of the comedy lounge, I couldn't help but smile and think about how my day started.

The morning was spent lazing in bed, recovering from the huge dinner and too many drinks to count the day before. The food, alcohol, and sunshine all day, mixed with the gentle rocking of the ship, created the perfect atmosphere for a deep and restful night's sleep and an even more relaxing morning.

I would have still been peacefully sleeping if I hadn't been awakened with some of the best loving possible. I couldn't believe he wasn't still dead to the world as well; but all notions of me sleeping were pushed aside as soon as my husband pushed inside.

It had to be the warm Caribbean sunshine streaming into our stateroom that had him up so early, or maybe it was the realization we were on the last day of our cruise. Whatever it was that had gotten into him so early in the morning, he ended up giving it to me. Twice.

After waiting a few minutes to allow my body to return to earth and for the convulsions to subside, I was wide awake and ready to start the day. We showered and went downstairs for a quick breakfast before getting off the ship to enjoy our final few hours in the Bahamas.

It was absolutely gorgeous outside, as if created just for us to enjoy. The sky was the perfect backdrop for all of the fun-in-the-sun activities that we ended up doing. There wasn't a cloud in sight as we snorkeled in the crystal clear waters washing up against the powder-white sand.

We strolled along the beach, holding hands, enjoying the scenery and each other. We browsed through the marketplace where vendors haggled with tourists, shouted out to potential customers, and entertained the crowds for tips.

After buying souvenirs for our friends, family, and coworkers, we returned to the ship. We wanted to be back before it was time to weigh anchor and head out. The ship was setting sail on time whether we were on board or not. As beautiful as the Bahamas was, I had no inclination to be stuck there.

Back on board, we went straight to the room. While Dante relaxed on the balcony, I took a much needed shower to wash off the salt water and all of the sand that had somehow manage to get into every crack and crevice of my body. That task completed,

I collapsed into the bed for a much needed nap, falling asleep the instant my head touched the pillow.

A few hours later, my growling stomach was the alarm that forced me to wake up. I looked over at the clock beside the bed and saw it was time for dinner. I awakened Dante and we both got dressed and headed upstairs to the dining room. For our meals tonight, I chose the broiled Australian lamb chop entrée, while Dante, a steak lover if there ever was one, settled on the Beef Carpaccio.

Our stomachs full, we decided to spend the rest of the evening enjoying more of the ship's nighttime activities. Thus far on cruise, we had visited the casino, gone shopping, played trivia, and I even managed to get Dante to get up in front of a group of strangers and sing karaoke with me.

As I thought about all of the things that we had done, I recalled our evening the night before. We had gone to the theater with the intention of watching a show, but it wasn't the performers on the stage that entertained us. Instead, I felt like it was me who was the main attraction for the night as I opened up and shared my deepest secrets.

We came upon a poster advertising the ship's comedy lounge so we decided to head there. We were soon walking inside the small auditorium located at the rear of the ship. Just as we found our seats, the lights came up and the host announced that next one would begin after a fifteen minute intermission.

"You want to stay and wait or leave and go do something else?" Dante asked, bringing me back to the present.

I hadn't heard much of anything because I had been in my own world thinking about the things still unsaid and unresolved with our future.

"No, let's stay here. I need a good laugh," I said, getting the attention of one of the many waiters that were seemingly everywhere on the ship. I wondered just how much alcohol they stored for the cruise as it seemed that there was a bar of some sort tucked into every nook and cranny of the ship.

I handed him my empty glass before ordering another mojito. Dante also ordered another drink before we settled back into our seats, relaxing in each other's company, watching people enter and leave the club—killing time before the show started.

I was enjoying this time with Dante. These precious moments together were more important than ever to me because I didn't know if or when this would come to an end. I had opened up to him these last few days and shared so much of myself. I knew I needed to tell him about my pain, my past, and my desires, because a part of me hoped that by being honest and transparent with him, that would open the door for him to do the same with me. So far, that had not been the case.

The waiter returned with our drinks and just as I was taking the first sip, I saw her. She had just come into the club with two other women from her group. I don't know what it was, but I could not help myself. Her sensuality was a magnet for my hunger, drawing me to her. Instinctively, I knew I had to keep my distance. I knew that I could not let her get too close because

I had more than an inkling as to what would occur and I could not allow that to happen. I had to fight against that happening at all costs.

She was dressed in a white and black striped sleeveless, fitted dress that hugged her frame. Once again, I found myself watching her as she gracefully walked to a booth a few feet from ours.

Seated almost 15 feet away, I could not understand why I was still able to feel the heat radiating from her as if she was standing next to me. I tried my best not to, but I had been watching her every night at dinner. I even found myself searching for her and no matter how hard I tried, my eyes sought her out. There was something innately sexy, something I couldn't put into words, that kept taking me back to places that I thought were well buried in my past.

I forced myself to turn away, taking a sip of my third mojito for the evening, trying to use the refreshing kick of the minty mixture to wash her out of my mind. I turned to Dante and saw that he had been studying me and now wore a puzzled expression on his face.

"You know her?"

I choked on my drink. I didn't know he'd been watching me once again. First at the airport and now here tonight.

"No, I don't. I just remember her from the dining room earlier," I answered, trying to sound as nonchalant as possible. "I noticed her outfit. It's cute, don't you think?"

"Oh, okay," he answered, a skeptical frown creasing his face as he sipped his Long Island iced tea. "You were staring at her with this weird look on your face. But yeah, her outfit's nice, I guess. It looks good on her."

Even knowing that Dante saw me, I still couldn't control myself as I turned in her direction yet again. This time, however, I was shocked to see that she was staring back at me with the sexiest, almost devious smile playing on her lips.

An intense warmth settled over my body as we continued to make eye contact. I turned away briefly to face the stage, welcoming the distraction from the show's host to take another huge swallow of my drink.

I could feel the mojitos working their dark magic, loosening my already tenuous grip on my self-control. I instantly knew that I had to get away from there, quickly.

An idea popped into my mind as to the perfect escape without hopefully arousing too much curiosity from Dante. "Hey! How about we go dancing, baby?" I said and stood in front of him, wiggling my hips, offering my hands in invitation for him to join me.

"Dancing? Huh? The show's about to start. I thought you wanted to stay?" he asked, his head moving left and right, following the rhythm of my gyrations like a cobra swaying to the snake charmer's flute.

"I changed my mind. C'mon, baby. Let's find the club. I think it's on this level," I said, picking up my drink and quickly draining it in several long gulps. I grabbed his hand and pulled him behind me, leading the way out of the lounge.

We knew we were heading in the right direction as the pulsing bass of dance music became increasingly louder the closer we got. Dante held the door open for me as we entered the crowded space. The dance floor in the center of the club was already filled with people bouncing to the beat.

I went straight to the middle of the floor and began moving, feeling the flow, letting myself get lost in the music. I felt a familiar pair of strong hands on my hips and backed into Dante as we moved together, swaying in sensual rhythm to the latest hip-hop tracks.

I lost all awareness of time as we swayed close to each other, enjoying the energy given off by the partygoers around us. Everyone was charged by the deep bass of the bone vibrating sound system and the blinding intensity of the flashing, psychedelic lights flickering throughout the club.

The DJ had been expertly mixing the music, and at that moment, slowed the tempo, putting on one of my favorite songs. Hearing the first few notes of the track, I closed my eyes, turned, and started dancing with my back to Dante. I moved back and forth, feeling a body move in front of me, swaying side-to-side, matching my movements, transforming our sensuous duo into an erotic trio as we moved in wordless, synced rhythm.

We had never been closer than five feet to each other at any given time before, but I knew it was her. I didn't need to open my eyes to verify this to be true. I could smell her scent. I could feel her energy. I knew.

As if reading my thoughts, she moved in even closer to me, her breasts pressing against mine, our bodies so close I could feel her breath on my cheek. I knew there was no turning back and I succumbed to the music, fell captive to her touch, and surrendered to the moment.

23

Dante

I paused and looked at the drop of sweat that had just fallen from my brow and splashed on to the back of our new friend. My eyes moved downward, following the deep arch and finally settling on her sumptuous behind.

I was positioned behind her, my hands gripping her hips, my strokes synchronized so that I pulled her back to me as the force of my thrusts pushed her away.

Just before reaching my peak, I stopped and withdrew from her, pausing to allow the mounting sensation of pleasure to subside. In that brief lull, I surveyed the room around me and was struck with just how surreal things appeared. From my vantage point, standing at the edge of the bed, I looked across the body down in front of me and directly into Celeste's eyes. She was gazing at me, and we stared at each other for a few moments. She let out a low moan, her eyes rolling into the back of her head before her eyelids fluttered closed, her body twitching at the pleasure she was receiving.

I once again admired the sumptuous curve of the rear end hovering in front of me. I was amazed that I was in this position, doing what I was doing. I felt like I was playing the role of the leading man in an intense triple-x movie being filmed somewhere in Hollywood. Even in the darkened room, the dim lights causing everything to be draped in shadows, I could still clearly trace the sensual lines of our new friend's body.

My eyes roamed over the woman's figure, from her supple behind, to her shoulders, and down to the tousled mane on her head which was currently buried between my wife's thick thighs that were spread eagle in the bed.

Enjoying the smooth sounds of Janet Jackson's "Anytime, Anyplace" which barely drowned out the moans coming from the two women, I could not help but be amazed at how it felt our situation, now being enhanced by the sexy songstress emotionally crooning about not giving a damn what they think, was the culmination of a whirlwind chain of events. Beginning with us leaving the dining room, and going from the comedy lounge to the nightclub before us finally ending up in our bed. *This is the stuff most guys fantasize about,* I thought as I watched how they tenderly interacted with each other. This was no fantasy however, as their enthusiastic exhalations emphasized how all too real this experience was.

I studied Celeste, her face a portrait of ecstasy, her body shivering with the magical manipulations of Desiré's tongue. I shook my head at the fact that never in a million years would I have imagined we would have another woman in bed with us, but here we were.

I had seen Desiré several times throughout the course of the cruise. In fact, it was impossible not to notice her. Her pecan-brown skin, toned body, shoulder-length curly hair, and alluring smile made her stand out like a lantern in a darkened room. I'm sure she had gotten Celeste's attention as well because our new friend sat at a table only a few feet away from ours every night at dinner. I remember Celeste's reaction the first time our friend came into the dining room and now, here she was, in our room dining on Celeste.

I reflected on how my wife reacted when she saw Desiré come into the comedy lounge earlier that evening. I was confused at first, especially at how Celeste's entire mood changed. Reflecting back on it now, I realized she had been trying to put distance between the two of them. That was the only explanation I could think of as to why she suggested we leave the comedy show and go to the nightclub instead. Her efforts were in vain, because like a cheetah chasing down a gazelle, our new friend had pursued Celeste, found her in the nightclub, and pounced. She had moved in for the sexual kill, hooking her artfully painted nails into Celeste's body, effectively ripping down the walls of resistance.

Celeste and I had been in the club dancing, or should I say grinding, on the dance floor when all of a sudden this woman came up and joined us. We were moving to the slow, pulsing beat of a hip-hop track when she suddenly appeared. Her provocative movements as she danced back-and-forth in front of Celeste were absolutely hypnotizing. Her body pressed in close, both of them seemingly in a trance, dancing together.

As the three of us moved, we no longer heard the music, dancing instead to our own rhythm. I watched our new friend, becoming increasingly aroused by her expressions, the subtle looks of lust seeming to have overtaken her. I couldn't see Celeste's face, but I instinctively knew her countenance reflected the same.

Our new friend's gaze shifted away from Celeste and focused on me. She held my eyes, swaying slowly before moving in and kissing my wife, never taking her eyes off me. We never stopped moving, continuing our slow, side-to-side sway to our manufactured rhythm, all the while her kissing Celeste and Celeste slowly grinding on me.

The force of the blood rushing into my manhood as I experienced this would have made Niagara Falls jealous. I wasn't sure where the evening was heading, but as I watched both women engage in their deep, passionate kiss, I knew we all needed to quickly go somewhere much more private. I whispered this suggestion in Celeste's ear and she silently nodded her agreement. Buoyed by her consent, I turned and led the way out of the club, Celeste in the middle holding her love with her left hand, pulling her lust in tow with her right.

We left the club, heading to our room to take our activities to even higher levels. Having to stop and wait for the elevator to take us to the eighth deck, I used that brief delay to make introductions. I told her our names before asking our new friend for hers.

She hesitated briefly before answering in a breathy voice dripping with sensuality, "Desiré."

As the elevator bell rang, I reflected on our conversation in the theater. Desire. That had been the word Celeste had used to describe her feelings for other women. She told me about the desires that she kept hidden, unsure of how to broach the subject.

The doors slid open in front of us to reveal an empty elevator car. I swept my arm in front of me, gesturing for the ladies to enter. Once inside, I leaned against the wall in the corner of the open space and observed my wife and Desiré. Like cage fighters before a brawl, we had all retreated to the far corners of the elevator as we eyed each other. No words were spoken on the short ride up and the subsequent walk down the hallway to our stateroom.

Now, less than thirty minutes later, I sat back and observed them together. Desiré's tongue, a brush, painting pleasure with each master stroke on Celeste's deliciously edible canvas. As arousing as it was to watch, it was at that moment I was able to put two and two together. I reached an understanding of what Celeste was telling me last night. Her past and all of the things she had been through, all of the things she tried to suppress were stirred by her encounter with the TSA agent. Now as we played in the pleasure playground that was our new friend's body, all of the pent up feelings she had been trying to repress were able to be released. Celeste had been like a person starving away on a desert island. She had all of the water she could drink, but she needed food. She needed to sexual sustenance.

I looked down at Celeste, her eyes locked shut as she enjoyed being devoured. Watching her, I couldn't help but think about the mistake I had made and the messed up situation I had brewing back home in Charlotte. My gaze drifted to Desiré and I was struck by the fact that I was having sex with a woman who wasn't my wife. Again. I wondered how this would affect things once we returned home. My mind swirled as I tried to process everything that was happening.

Celeste's rising moans as Desiré orally continued to skillfully push her buttons, caused me to break out of the fog of my thoughts and refocus on the task at hand. *I'll worry about Charlotte when I get back there,* I thought as I repositioned myself behind Desiré. Aggressively reentering her, I paused briefly to savor the sound of her loud gasp of pleasure. I then began moving my hips, slowly increasing the speed and intensity of each thrust. I found the perfect balance of power and pace, relishing the sensation of Desiré's body meeting mine as she matched me stroke for stroke. With our three-link carnal chain once again connected, we energetically traveled a rollercoaster ride of ecstasy until we all reached the crest of our climax almost simultaneously. Unable to hold back the building pleasure aching to be released, I finally succumbed to the feeling and exploded with a guttural scream I was sure could be heard by everyone on the ship.

Every nerve ending on my body was on fire as I skyrocketed to heights of pleasure that before tonight never knew existed. I had never experienced anything as powerful as what we had just done. My eyes slowly refocused and I looked over at my wife who lay spent from whatever heights she had just visited. We stared at each other, sharing a smile that spoke of our love, our happiness, our bond.

I didn't want this beautiful event to be the grand finale of our love story. I desperately hoped that when I shared my secret with her, she wouldn't leave me. There was no way I could love anyone the way that I loved her.

My energy drained, both mentally and physically, I collapsed on the bed between them, basking in the moment, never wanting this feeling to end.

24

Michal

As I headed back to my room, making what I have secretly come to call my 'Walk of Fame', I was hit with the sudden urge to make a quick detour. I was tempted to hang a banner across the Lido deck reading, 'Mission Accomplished' just like the overzealous former President had done several years ago on the deck of an aircraft carrier. Unlike him however, I had done exactly what I set out to achieve with my covert, carnal activities. I had set three objectives and here I was, triumphantly headed back to my room knowing I had met each of them.

One guy. One girl. One couple. Those were the entrees on my menu of mischief for the cruise and I had dabbled in all three of those delicious courses. Greg, Martina, along with both Celeste and Dante were the people I had honed in on, the prey Desiré, my aggressive alter ego had hunted, had seized, had devoured.

Before I had even boarded the plane in Houston, I knew what I wanted to do. On my way to the ship, all I could think about was the fact that I didn't know how I would go about things or with whom I would do them. I didn't know when it would happen with each of the people I had selected or where exactly things would go down. That was another part of the thrill—the unknown factor. I relished the thought of how my unnamed partners would look, how they would feel, how they would taste. From the minute I left my home heading the to the airport, the anticipation was deliciously intoxicating, my appetite increasing the closer I got to the ship.

This wasn't my first such sexual scavenger hunt, but it was definitely the best. This installment presented a challenge because it took place within the confines of a cruise ship. Compared to my previous adventures on my trips to Washington, DC and Las Vegas where I had the option to roam the entire city, this love boat proved to be an absolutely amazing experience.

The bottom line was just as I had done on those other trips, I accomplished exactly what I set out to. What made it even sweeter was that I had closed out my quest right before the cruise ended, as we would be pulling back into the Miami harbor early tomorrow morning.

I stopped in front of the elevator and checked the time, surprised to see that it was going on two A.M. *Damn, time truly does fly when you're having fun,* I thought with a sly grin spreading across my face as I recalled the activities of the last few hours.

I waited for the elevator and replayed the evening, which began innocently enough with my girls and I roaming aimlessly around the ship. At that time, in the back of my mind, I didn't think I was going to achieve my goal for the cruise. All of that changed when we entered the comedy lounge and I saw Celeste and Dante sitting across the room. The instant I locked eyes with Celeste, I knew the goddess Oshun was smiling down on me because I knew exactly where the evening would lead.

I chuckled as I watched her trying to fight against the inevitable by rushing out, dragging Dante behind her. All that served to do was make the night even that much more interesting. A lioness on the hunt, I politely excused myself and left my girls behind to pursue my prey of passion.

I lost sight of them for a while, the crowds of people milling around providing them with cover. When I heard, or should I say felt, the music from the nightclub, I instinctively knew that I had found them. Sure enough, there they were, dancing together in the middle of the dance floor. The moment was there and I didn't waste any more time. I walked on to the dance floor and pressed my body against hers, matching their rhythm, rocking to-and-fro, dancing with them.

After a few minutes, the unspoken understanding between us having been established, we left the club and headed to their room to act upon our amorous agreement. Once there, I had the threesome experience I had been yearning to enjoy for the past two years. Sadly, I knew all too well from some past exploits with couples that playing with them can end terribly. One minute things would be going perfectly and then in the blink of an eye, the whole mood would be destroyed when egos became bruised, allowing jealousy and insecurity to enter, forcing passion and energy to leave.

Luckily, that was not the case with these two. The love they had for each other was evident in the way they interacted with each other and in the way they shared me. That love translated into how they handled me, his heavier touch being counterbalanced by her gentler one. The different sensations that came from each of them drove me absolutely crazy, making the entire encounter incredibly intense.

As the evening progressed, I deduced that this was their first time engaging in something like this. It wasn't just his tentative approach or their overall body language giving this away, but it was also evident in the fact that he didn't have any of the necessary protection for the night's activities. I had come prepared, however, and that hurdle was quickly cleared.

There was minimal communication between us three but as soon as we got to the room, she instantly became aggressive, pushing me back on the bed, soft kisses leading to her exploring every part of me. I was momentarily confused but slowly understood why she had been running from me. I knew all too well about holding back desires. When you finally got to release all of those pent up cravings, the appetite, having been starved up to that point, is beyond voracious and all semblance of control is lost as you try to feed it.

So wrapped up in my thoughts, I was startled when I realized I had arrived at my door. I had been walking in a trance, thinking about last night and how it had been the perfect way to close out the cruise. Not only did they allow me to meet my goal, but being with them had been a pleasurable experience as well.

I shook my head to clear the still vivid images from my mind. I slid my keycard through the slot, shrugging because all good things must come to an end. As much as I dreaded the thought, a part of me welcomed the notion that I would be heading back home soon to Houston.

Tip-toeing into the dark room, I gently pushed the door closed, trying to be as quiet as possible so as to not wake Kendra. I was sure she would be sleeping as it was well past two-thirty. With the door closed behind me, I stood still in the entrance, listening for the sounds of her heavy breathing, hoping to confirm that she was in fact sleeping.

This was not to be. "Welcome back," she said dryly. "Did you have fun?" she asked, her voice, knife-edged, slicing through the quiet space of the dark room, the sarcasm in her tone making her question even sharper as it cut into me. She had made no attempt to mask the venom dripping from each word of her derisive inquiry. I was glad the room was dark because I would not have been able to deal with the judgmental expression I knew was plastered on her face.

I closed my eyes, attempting to gather my patience before speaking to her. Up to now, I had been having a great night, a phenomenal night in fact, and I was not going to allow her pettiness to ruin it.

"As a matter of fact, I did have fun, thanks. How about you?" I replied, ducking into the bathroom before she could answer the question, ensuring there would be no more conversation between us. I was fast, but not fast enough to miss the scornful, judgment laden, "mmmm hmmmm" she threw at me.

Safely locked inside, the thin door providing a barrier of sorts from Kendra's negativity, I took that moment of solitude to gather myself. Staring at my reflection in the mirror, I stood there for several minutes, peering deeply into my own eyes, alone with myself, alone with my thoughts, alone with my truths.

A smile of satisfaction spread across my face as I thought about the past few days. The smile turned into a grin as I reached for the hot water faucet, turning it on to wash up and prepare for bed. The trip was over and tomorrow would be back to my normal life, back to reality.

25

Dante

The light mist of the cool sea spray settled on my skin as I sat alone in one of the deck chairs on the small balcony outside of our room. I used the peaceful moment in the quiet, early morning air to reflect on everything that had happened the last few days. So far, each day had been filled with one surprise after another.

The sky was a dull, hazy gray as the sun was still several hours away from rising. As hesitant as I had been about going on this cruise, I now didn't want it to end. From the sexy start in the airport to the fantasy finale last night, this vacation would be one I would never forget.

I slipped back into the room and took a sip from one of the two glasses of orange juice on the tray that had been delivered by room service a few moments earlier. The plates were loaded with several strips of bacon, two blueberry muffins, and juice. I marveled at the level of service we had received all weekend. It didn't matter if it was a phone call at four in the morning or four in the afternoon, a few minutes after you hung up, a server was knocking on the door delivering your order.

I unfolded a napkin and spread it over the food before passing the bed, pausing to look at my wife who was wrapped up in the sheets sleeping. My heart warmed with love and affection for her as I thought about how she had opened her heart, sharing her deepest, most painful secrets of her past with me. I listened to her, felt her fears, embraced her vulnerability as she lay herself emotionally bare in front of me. She allowed me to see a part of her past that no one else had ever been granted entry.

I went back to the balcony and sat, knowing that before this ship touched the dock in Miami, I would do the same with her.

"Can't sleep?" Celeste asked, startling me out of my thoughts. I had not heard her get up from the bed and come up behind me.

In the faint light cast from the lamp in the room behind us, I could see she had on a pair of my shorts and one of my tank tops. Each piece of clothing was huge and hanging off her, making her seem childlike in appearance.

She was carrying the plate of bacon and chewing on a slice as she joined me on the balcony. As long as I had known her, she could never pass up bacon. The strange thing was that she rarely, if ever, cooked bacon at home; however, whenever we went out to eat, she never missed the opportunity to indulge herself.

"Nah, I couldn't, Mrs. Wright. I came out here to chill for a bit. I was sitting here thinking about how nice this cruise has been. I can honestly say I really enjoyed myself," I said, reaching over and plucking one of the thick strips right out of her hand.

My action resulted in her giving me a stare that could have melted steel.

"Be glad I love you, because the last person that took bacon from me, they still haven't found the body," she said as she held the plate to her chest protectively.

"Whatever," I said, reaching over and taking another slice. "Now what? I'm not scared of you...that much."

We exchanged a few mean scowls before we both burst into laughter. No other woman had ever made me feel the wealth of emotions that she does. Her sense of humor never failed to make me laugh even when she drove me crazy with her headstrong attitude.

We had shared the most intense experience not even two hours ago when Desiré came into our bed. Even that didn't ease the turmoil inside me; I had no idea how she would react once I told her my secret. I hoped and prayed we would be able to make it through the next few minutes, the next few days, the next few months after I opened up to her.

My hands were clammy with sweat and my body temperature spiked as I contemplated the exact words to say to her. Here we were, together on this narrow balcony, the only things between us being a small table and my huge secret. The crisp ocean air, cool and comfortable only a few minutes ago, now seemed as hot as if the midday sun was suddenly beaming down directly on me. I picked up my juice and quickly drained the glass in a few quick gulps. I hoped that the cool liquid would help to calm me, but it offered no relief from the nervous heat broiling me from within.

"I'll be back, babe. I'm going to get some water," I said, using the empty glass as an excuse to escape.

"Is everything okay?" she asked, her voice suddenly filled with concern.

"Yeah. I'm good. Still drained from our escapade last night," I said, giving her a quick wink.

The soft brown complexion of her face became even richer as she blushed. "If that's the case, bring me back some as well," she said with a giggle.

"I got you," I said, going from the balcony and back into the room. I stood in front of the cooler, my mind a blur as I played out in my head all of the different ways Celeste might react. I imagined her blowing up, pouring the water over my head, and probably even trying to throw me over the balcony when I told her about my infidelity.

Maybe she would have the opposite reaction and not say anything at all. Not say anything to me as we disembarked the ship in Miami. Not say anything to me as we boarded our plane to go back home to Charlotte. Not say anything to me as she went to the courthouse to file for a divorce, our once happy marriage ending in the nosiest silence.

Taking a deep breath, I knew that I couldn't stall any longer. I took out two bottles of water and went back to the balcony.

Celeste happily munched on another strip of bacon as she gazed out at the never-ending murkiness of the ocean stretching out to meet the even darker gloom of the horizon. I took a mental picture of my wife, trying to lock in this image of pure beauty in front of me. I wanted to remember the way the lamp light behind her reflected off her exposed shoulders. I wanted to remember the curve of her full lips that seemed to have a perpetual smile, a smile that I feared I would never see again.

I placed a bottle on the table beside her, the dull thud of the heavy plastic hitting the table's surface causing her to turn to me. Her radiant smile froze me, making me hesitate, draining me of my will. I didn't want to break her heart.

I sat beside her and closed my eyes for a few seconds, praying for guidance. My divine plea made, amen said, resolve restored, I took a deep breath, opened my eyes, and looked into hers. She had been watching me, the curiosity evident on her face, trying to figure out what was going on.

"Dante? Is everything okay?" she asked hesitantly, a strip of bacon stopped midway on its journey from the plate to her mouth.

I allowed her question to linger in the air between us for several moments before I spoke. "Imani," was the one word answer I gave her, my voice barely above a whisper as I told her my daughter's name. I had never said Imani's name, much less told anyone about her up to this point. Not my parents, my friends, my pastor. No one knew about her. Until now.

26

Celeste

The moment I had been waiting on for so long was finally here. "Imani? Who...who is that?" I asked, still holding the strip of bacon which was now shaking in my trembling fingers as I awaited his response. I took a deep breath and braced myself, summoning the courage to accept whatever truths or decipher whatever lies he was about to put forth in front of me.

"Imani. She's...she's my daughter," he said quietly, staring down at his bare feet as he repeated the name. "She's the result of a stupid decision that I made right before we got married."

All I could do was stare at him. I couldn't speak, couldn't blink, couldn't breathe. It was as if he had sucked up all of the oxygen in the world with that one statement. He held his head up, staring at me, his eyes pleading for understanding—for forgiveness.

The anger I had been carrying for all these months was finally lifted. Suddenly, sublimely, I felt my spirit lighten as the painful shackles of betrayal and dishonesty which had been weighing down my heart, were finally loosened ever so slightly.

"Oh, okay," I said with a rueful chuckle, my features softening. "I thought that was the name of your girlfriend. Or your side chick, mistress, or whatever the hell they're called these days."

The incredulous expression on his face bespoke the fact that this was obviously not the reaction he had been expecting. I knew he was trying to figure out what was happening, trying to understand what was going through my head. I smiled and just shook my head as I watched him quickly glance down at the table and the balcony around us, no doubt trying to make sure that there weren't any sharp knives or heavy blunt objects within my reach. I knew it had taken a lot for him to tell me about his child so he had probably prepared himself for the worst.

"No, not even," he said sadly. "As crazy as it sounds, I wish that were the case though. If it was just another woman, that would be completely different. A side chick, well, I could leave her and never have to see her again. A child, my daughter, well… that's not so easy. She's here to stay."

I nodded my head in silent agreement. I brought the strip of bacon up to my lips, nibbling on it as I considered where Dante and I found ourselves, and more importantly, where we were headed. The sound of the wind rushing by mixed with the waves crashing as the ship cut through them could not overpower the deafening silence lingering between us.

Every time I thought about how this scene would play out, I had envisioned myself yelling, crying, hitting him, kicking him, doing anything to let him feel all of the pain I had been living with ever since I discovered his secret. Now, finally, we had arrived at the moment of truth, and instead of being filled with intense anger, I was overcome with a feeling of peace. Was it the bacon? The afterglow that I was still experiencing from our evening of pleasure with Desiré. Whatever the case might be, I was just too emotionally drained to react and all I could do was stare at him.

The dead air between us ceased to be as he took a deep breath before opening up and telling me what happened between him and her. Ebonie. The woman he cheated on me with. The mother of his child. He proceeded to rip open the dark cloud hovering over us and let his truths rain down as he told me the entire story. He spoke of how they had met and the things that they had done, not sparing any of the sordid details.

I listened quietly, turning away from him and sitting rigidly in my chair, eyes staring straight ahead into the dull gray horizon. His words stole my appetite and it took all I had to hold back the tears. My mind went back to the child that was growing inside me so many years ago. A large part of me died the moment that baby did. It wasn't until I met Dante that I learned to love again. Listening to him talk about his betrayal of my love, my trust, cut me down to my very being.

He finally finished talking, the silence once again enveloping us as I closed my eyes and processed my feelings. After several minutes, I said quietly, "I already knew about your child, Dante."

"What?" he asked in disbelief, his head whipping around to face me. "You know about her? But…but…how?" he sputtered.

I laughed quietly as I picked up the bottle of water from the table and twisted off the cap. I was sure that of all the things he had anticipated me saying, that piece of information was most definitely not on that list.

I raised the bottle to my lips, the cool liquid refreshing me, soothing me. I took several deep gulps before I spoke again. "Dante, I handle the money," I said matter-of-factly, "If I see anything out of the ordinary effecting the business of our household, then it's my duty to get to the bottom of it. You worked all of that overtime, gone almost every Saturday, yet your paychecks stayed about the same. That just wasn't adding up."

I heard him let out a loud groan as he reached up and slapped his palm to his forehead. I guess he thought he had covered his tracks, but obviously that wasn't the case.

"So anyway," I continued, ignoring his antics. "I called the payroll office at Sysco and talked to one of the clerks that I knew from way back when she used to work in the accounting office at the hospital. She did some checking and that's how I found out you diverted some of your check into a separate bank account. All of your passwords are the same so it was too easy for me to check your bank statements online. I didn't know if you had a son or a daughter or even who the child's mother was. All I knew was that you writing checks for child support and had recently begun doing so."

"Why didn't you say something?" he asked in a tone filled with surprise. "I can't believe you knew about this and didn't say anything."

"I was waiting on you to come clean," I said. "In fact, I'd given you until the end of the year."

"The end of the year? And what if I hadn't said anything?"

"Then I was going to leave you."

"Leave me?" he asked, his eyebrows shooting up in surprise at my statement.

"Yes, Dante," I said coolly, my voice firm so that he would know that I meant every word that I spoke. "As hard as it was and still is to deal with, I love you. You know about all of the crap I've gone through. It wasn't until I met you that I thought I could be able to love someone again. Well, I opened up, let you in, and now I can't let you go. I thought I could, but I can't. And it's all because I love you. That means I take all of the garbage that comes along with being with you and being your wife. But if you couldn't be honest with me, I was going to leave you. Please believe it. If the end of the year came without you doing so, then my new year's resolution was to divorce you. I've been through too much and I wasn't going to be with a man that could keep such a big secret from me."

We sat quietly for several moments before he finally spoke, his voice quavering slightly as he asked, "So what do we do now, Celeste?"

I thought about the question before taking a deep breath and responded softly, "Well, when we get home, we'll sit down, come up with a game plan, and work through this together. I'm not even going to lie, It won't be easy for me, but I'm going to have to deal with it."

I watched his body slumped as he heard my words. "Baby, I'm so sorry," he said, his eyes filling with tears as he reached across the table to take my hands in his. "I know I messed up, but I promise you I'll never hurt you like this again."

My thumb lightly kneading the top of his knuckles. "I believe you," I said finally. *I believe you, but the real question is: will I ever be able to trust you again?* I thought as I gently squeezed his hand.

He got up from his seat and got on his knees in front of my chair. Now closer to me, he leaned forward, gently holding my face in his hands and gazing deeply into my eyes before giving me a long, gentle kiss.

As our kiss slowly ended, I saw the tears running down his cheeks. He seemed exhausted, as if he had just finished running a marathon. I knew he had been holding in his secret for so long, just as I had been bearing the hefty weight of his infidelity inside as well.

"I'm so sorry. So sorry," he sobbed, repeating his heartfelt pleading over and over. I held him close to my chest as he cried, releasing tears of pain and frustration.

27

Greg

I glanced up at the television monitor that was hanging over the row of seats in the Miami International Airport. I groaned at the highlights from the past weekend's NFL games after seeing that my Patriots had lost yet again, this time to the Carolina Panthers. I shook my head and turned away from the screen in disgust.

I focused my attention on the bustling activity of the airport concourse, scanning the area around me, my eyes finally settling on the restaurant where Angel and Cory sat talking with each other. They had left the group when they had decided, or rather Cory had made the decision for them, to go and get coffee.

I sat slouched in one of the uncomfortable gray, plastic chairs that had to have been designed by some dastardly sadomasochist somewhere, and watched Angel. I thought about how my feelings for her had changed over the span of only four days. Before the cruise, I stumbled around in confusion, trying to come to grips with why she had ended things between us. For ten months, we had gotten so close, establishing what I thought was the foundation of a special relationship. I knew she had her ways when it came to money and expected the finer things in life, but her beauty, intelligence, sensuality was unlike anything I had ever experienced.

Since my divorce over seven years ago from my ex-wife, Charlene, I was a notorious bachelor. The idea of being with the same woman for more than a week at a time had never crossed my mind, so I never thought I would ever have any real feelings about a woman. I had grown comfortable being single, but that was before Angel kicked in the door to my world, entered my heart, and turned my whole life upside-down.

I watched the two of them sitting at a table, a huge grin on Angel's face before she leaned her head back and laughed enthusiastically at something Cory said. I shook my head in displeasure at this. I didn't like the guy before we left Atlanta, and after being in closer proximity to him these last few days, I liked him even less now. The cruise only reinforced my hunch that there was something off about him, but I still couldn't quite put my finger on it on just what it was.

Was I feeling this way about him because I was jealous? I wondered as I returned my attention to the television monitor to distract myself. *To hell with both of them. They deserve each other,* I told myself firmly as I checked my watch and thanked God that we would soon be getting on the plane.

Quickly tiring of watching the endless loop of news, sports, and weather reports cycling on the monitor, I decided to get up and take a walk to clear my head.

"I'll be back," I said to Evan sitting next to me.

"The flight's going to be boarding in a few minutes," he said, looking up from his iPhone where he had been furiously texting someone.

"I'll be back in time," I said over my shoulder as I walked away from him.

I wondered what the future held for me as I roamed through the crowded airport with no real destination in mind. Evan and I would be moving forward with opening our shop almost the second we got back to Atlanta. I was beyond excited at the prospect of being a business owner. After all of the things that I had been through in my life, this latest endeavor was truly a dream come true.

The sound of the airport intercom cut through my thoughts as an attendant announced the boarding of an American Airlines flight going to Houston. I glanced over at the group of people that had gotten up and walked over to the gate to get in line to board the plane. I slowed my pace when I saw that one of those passengers standing in line was Desiré. I couldn't stop the smile spreading across my face as I remembered how we initially met and our subsequent encounter the following night. She must have felt my eyes on hers because she turned toward me. Our eyes locked for a few seconds and then she gave me that seductive smile of hers, winked at me, right before going through the entrance of the jetway leading to her plane.

Watching her leave, something inside of me clicked. I didn't know what it was, but I just felt different. I turned and headed back to the group to wait for our flight to board. My steps felt lighter, as if a weight had been lifted off my shoulders.

Before arriving at the waiting area, I veered off into the restroom to empty my bladder and wash my face in preparation for being on a plane for the next three hours. I would never use the lavatory on a plane because I don't care what nobody says, I was not going to get sucked into the toilet. I either used the restroom before I got on the plane or held it until I got off.

I handled my business and stopped at the water fountain outside of the restroom. As I stood up from drinking and turned to walk away, I almost ran right into Angel who had been standing there hovering over me.

"Hey, there," she said cheerfully, a huge smile plastered on her face.

"Whattup," I said dryly, stepping around her to go back to my seat.

"Hold on. I want to talk to you for a second," she said, reaching out, gently grabbing my forearm and pulling me back to her. The electricity from her touch shot through me, freezing me. Her soft fingers delicately squeezed my arm and she had a look in her eyes that I had never seen before.

"What's up?" I asked. *Had she been standing here waiting on me to get back so she could talk to me?* I asked myself, wondering just what she was up to.

"Umm...I just wanted to say that..." she stammered, looking over my shoulder in the direction of Cory, who was sitting at the far end of the waiting area. "I'll tell you now since you were busy when I went by your room the other night. I wanted to tell you that even though I'm with Cory, that doesn't mean that you and I still can't be friends. Although it seemed like you had already made a new friend the other night. But even that doesn't matter; I want you to know we can still see each other," she said, her voice trailing off as she stood there, rubbing her fingers seductively on my arm.

All I could do was stare at her, speechless. It was as if she had grown another head out of her shoulders. *Was she serious?* I couldn't believe she had the audacity to try me like this.

"Angel, that won't work...at all," I said with quiet emphasis, staring directly into her eyes to make sure she understood every word I was saying. "You made your decision. You told me on several occasions just what you wanted, but I didn't listen. It hurts, but you know what, I'm going to let you go. You wanted to be with Cory, so I'm going to let you do just that—be with Cory."

"But...I thought...you said...you said you loved me," she said, completely flustered. My flat out refusal of her indecent proposal was obviously not the reaction she had been expecting. For the few months we had been together, I had gone along with pretty much whatever she wanted. The only things preventing her from getting her way was my lack of funds or the secrecy of our situation. Observing her now, I was sure that my reaction was confusing to her, however, it was very liberating for me.

I looked over my shoulder and saw Cory get up from his seat, looking around as if trying to find her. I decided it was time to end this conversation because I didn't feel like having to lay hands on the dude in the middle of the airport.

"Look, I do love you, Angel," I said. "That's why I want you to be happy. Obviously I can't provide you with or do the things for you that he can, so to make things easier for you, I'm falling back."

With that, I turned away from her, not giving her a chance to respond nor prolong the conversation. I had said what I had to say. It irritated me that she wanted to have her cake and eat it, too. I had told her the truth. I did love her. I just loved myself more.

I had to close the chapter in my life called Angel. There was one thing that I had learned over the years—never backtrack. There was a reason why relationships ended, and backtracking in the hopes that things would be better the second time around never yielded encouraging results. I wanted nothing but positivity in my future, and I knew I would never get that if I kept messing around with her.

The gate agent announced our flight would begin boarding. I stood and picked up my bags, my heart light, my spirits uplifted. Not only had I made it through the cruise, but I was returning a better man. In a few hours, I would be back at home, ready to move forward with my life, wherever it would take me. I didn't know what the future held or who I might end up with. *Who knows, I might even run into Desiré again later down the road*, I thought as I took my place in line to board my flight home.

28

Celeste

*I*t felt so good to finally be able to stretch my legs after being cramped up on that plane all the way from Florida. For the flight home, I was dressed comfortably in a loose fitting jogging suit and tennis shoes, but it seemed that no matter what I tried, I just could not get relaxed.

As we deplaned and walked down the narrow jetway on our way to the baggage claim area, I was hit with a feeling of tremendous anxiety. Sadly, our vacation together was officially over and now it would be time to go to work. The more I thought about it, I wasn't really concerned about my job at the hospital. I was focused more on all of the other things swirling around in my head. Specifically, the many issues that would have to be addressed with Dante and myself.

As we walked through the bustling airport, I reflected on the previous few days. We had done so much together, shared so much with each other, opened ourselves up in areas I never thought we would. The physical acts of pleasure we explored was nothing compared to the emotional sharing that was exchanged. I knew that with everything out in the open, no longer hidden in the shadows of secrecy, our marriage now had a chance of surviving. I also knew it would require a lot of time, communication, and trust for us to get through this trying period, but I believed we would make it.

I was so glad Dante came clean with me and told me about his daughter. I had been wanting him to tell me for so long. Now that he had done just that however, I was more confused than ever. I wasn't sure if I could handle the fact he had cheated on me. How could I deal with being around the child? His daughter. The innocent proof of his indiscretion. Yes, I could rationalize it by saying she was conceived before we were married, but no amount of technicalities could change the fact that Dante stepped out, regardless of what phase our relationship may have happened to be in.

I listened to his explanation about what happened between him and her, how things had gone down, but I was still left with the lingering question: would it happen again? I knew he was remorseful and apologetic, having professed his love for me over and over again, but I still had to wonder if I could really trust him.

I was jarred back to reality by the driver of the passenger assistance cart blaring the horn as it rolled towards us. As I moved to the side to allow the cart carrying three elderly people to pass, I was suddenly struck with the thought that I knew nothing about her. A myriad of questions flooded my mind. *Who was the baby's mother? Was that really their one and only time? What if she changed her mind all of a sudden and wanted Dante to be more than just a monthly child support payment? It was only a matter of time that she would want more, wasn't it?*

The questions came at me so quickly that I barely had time to register one thought before violently being hit with another. My mind was reeling and I was barely able to focus on much of anything around me, however a blur of blue in my peripheral vision caught my attention. I glanced over and like a beacon cutting through the dense fog in my head, her face came into clarity. The TSA agent from a few days ago, the same agent that had stirred feelings in me that had long been dormant, was coming towards us. She had on large, red headphones covering her ears and was moving confidently through the crowd, taking long, graceful strides as she went upstream, moving against the tide of travelers heading out of the airport.

She walked right by me, oblivious to everything around her. I was surprised that she didn't burst into flames when she passed by because I'm sure I was putting out enough heat to make the sun envious.

Seeing her brought back memories of the things that I had shared with Dante. The things I had told him about my past that I thought I would never tell anyone, much less my husband.

Would we do something like that ever again, or was it just something about that woman, Desiré? How was Dante really feeling about what we had done? He had definitely enjoyed himself; however, he hadn't said anything else about it since last night. I'm sure that he might be distracted with the more weightier issues, namely his daughter, but it still didn't change the fact that I didn't know how he felt about everything that had went down last night.

Dante recognized the agent as well and turned to ask me, "Hey, Celeste. Wasn't that the sa-" He stopped abruptly as soon as he saw the expression on my face.

"What's wrong? You okay?" he asked with a mixture of curiosity and concern on his face.

"I'm fine," I snapped, quickening my pace so that I was a few steps in front of him. I was far from fine, in fact, I was a mess right now, a bundle of unfettered emotions being battered around by the events of the weekend along with my unknown future with Dante. It was causing me to feel as if I was spinning around in an emotional tornado.

"Fine, huh? You sure about that?" he asked sarcastically.

I couldn't believe he had the nerve to try and have an attitude with me. He quickly caught up with me, matching my strides, scrutinizing me before saying, "You looked stressed out. That's how you really look. You sure as hell don't look like someone returning from vacation, that's for sure."

His statement caused me to stop in my tracks, forcing the crowd that we were moving in to flow around us in order to continue on their way. Dante stopped walking as well, took a deep breath as he turned his head up to the ceiling as if praying for either patience, guidance, or both, before he turned around and came back to where I was standing.

"Celeste, look. I kno-," he began, but I cut him off before he could even get started. I was not in the mood to hear anything that he had to say.

"No Dante, you look," I said, trying to control the anger that was on the verge of boiling over. Even though we were standing in the middle of the concourse, I couldn't move any further until I let out the feelings bottled up inside of me.

"I don't think you fully understand what I'm feeling right about now," I said through clenched teeth. "I told you that I would stay with you and that we'll work things out between us, your daughter, and your baby-momma, but that doesn't mean I'll like it. I am beyond pissed with you right now. I'm angry as hell! Don't you get it? You betrayed me, Dante! You hurt me. So yes, dear husband, I am very stressed out."

"I understand," he said quietly, hanging his head. "I just thought that after our talk this morning we were going to work through things. I know it's going to be hard and I promise you, if I could take it all back, all of your pain, all of the stress, all of the hurt, I would. In a heartbeat I would."

I closed my eyes and took in a deep breath to calm myself before speaking again. "I don't know what the future holds for us, Dante. For the past six months, I've been planning on leaving you. I honestly didn't think you'd confess to cheating on me. You just told me everything this morning, so please don't think I can instantly adjust in only a few hours. I'm glad that you finally told me, but I'm still trying to deal with everything. I have to work through how I feel about you and this whole situation."

He stood there looking at me, not saying a word. Finally, he let go of the handle of the carry-on bag he was pulling before shucking out of his knapsack which had been slung over his shoulders. With his hands now free, he silently moved closer to me and pulled me into his arms.

At his soft touch, the simple gesture of reassurance that I needed more than I realized, the emotional dam burst and the tears flowed. He held me even closer to him, my head resting on his chest as my body racked with the powerful sobs tearing through me. He said nothing as my tears of hurt and sorrow soaked into his T-shirt.

I slowly calmed down as the relaxing smell of the faint traces of cologne lingering on his shirt plus his firm embrace soothed me. I didn't know how upset I really was and couldn't even pinpoint what it was exactly that had set off my hysterics. What I did know was that I felt better. I felt relieved.

"Baby, I know I messed up," he whispered softly into my ear. He slowly rubbed my back reassuringly as he spoke, his words gentle, his voice soothing. "I messed up big time, but I want you to know that I'm going to make it right. I promise you that. I love you and don't want to lose you. I know this won't be easy for you, it won't be easy for us, but I know we can make it through this. I know we can."

Could I trust him? Could I ever trust him again? I thought as his words washed over me. This same thought had been on a never-ending loop for the past few hours. I wanted to believe him, I needed to believe him. I had to believe him.

"I hope we can, too," I said, tilting my head up from his chest and looking up into his eyes. I was moved with the sincere love for me that I saw reflecting in them. I loved this man and I knew he loved me. Only time would tell if love would be enough to get us through the obstacles that lay in front of us.

"Come on, baby. Let's get out of here and go home," he said as he picked up our luggage and extended his free hand towards me.

I exhaled a sigh of frustration, inhaling a deep breath of hope before taking his outstretched hand in mine.

I told him on the ship this morning that we were going to work through things and it was now time to see if that indeed would be possible. Our vacation was over and now it was back to the real world and all of the problems that came along with it.

29

Dante

I watched as my wife dried her eyes with a Kleenex that she had pulled out of her purse. After having broken down into tears only a few moments ago, she had composed herself and was now noticeably calmer.

"Come on, baby. Let's get out of here and go home," I said as I picked up our bags before reaching out my free hand to her. As she took my hand in hers and we began walking, I thought about all of the things that I had done to get us to this point. I still couldn't believe my stupidity. I thought I had my tracks covered, but obviously that wasn't the case. My father had once warned me that no matter how slick you think you might be, your woman was even slicker and more importantly, was way smarter than you could ever be. Sooner or later, they will find out and uncover the truth, no matter how well you thought you had it covered or how deep you had it buried.

I was still in a daze from our earlier conversation and Celeste's revelations. There was no hesitation in her voice when she said she was going to leave me. Even now, as I recalled looking into her eyes, I knew she meant every word. I liked that. I could deal with a lot of character flaws in people because I know that no one is perfect. The one thing I could not deal with however, is a person I that could not trust. With that in mind, I knew that I had a lot of work to do to restore her trust in me. I was going to have to do everything possible to repair the bond of trust that I broke when I cheated on her. The more I thought about it, not only had I cheated on her, but I ended up with a child as a product of that ill-fated choice. A child that would always be to her a reminder of my stupid decision. I shook my head in frustration as I thought about the uphill battle that lay ahead of me.

As we walked through the terminal, I turned to one of the overhead television monitors just in time to catch the scores of the football games from the past weekend. I stopped walking to watch the highlights and pumped my fist when I saw that my Panthers had pulled out a close victory over the New England Patriots. With that win, I knew that we would be heading to the playoffs and be one step closer to the Super Bowl.

"C'mon, Dante," Celeste called over her shoulder. "Let's get home."

Home. That one word jarred me back to the reality I faced. That we faced. *How would things be when we got home?* I wondered as I trotted forward to catch up with my wife. So far, I was feeling optimistic that things would work out for the best between us, but who knows what might come up in the future.

I thought about the reaction that came over Celeste a few minutes ago when the TSA agent went by us. The woman seemed to be even sexier now than she did a few days ago when she subjected Celeste to the most erotic pat down procedure I had ever had the pleasure of witnessing. She hadn't noticed us, but there was no doubt Celeste noticed her. The subdued hostility she demonstrated when I tried to point the agent out as she passed by let me know she was not in the mood to talk about it at all.

I was more confused than ever. *All of the things we'd gone through, all of the secrets and emotions that we shared, were they for nothing? Now that we were back home, would all of it be forgotten? Would she retreat into herself and act as if nothing had happened between her and the agent? Would she act as if the night with Desiré didn't happen?* All of these thoughts swirled through my head as we walked out of the terminal.

As we stood outside of the busy airport, I embraced the familiar warmth of the North Carolina sunshine. We had been outside almost the entire weekend, so it wasn't like we had been cooped up indoors, but there was something reassuring about being home.

The shuttle that would take us to the parking garage where we had left the car pulled up to the curb and we climbed aboard. There was nothing said between us on the short ride and that worried me more than anything. I kept hoping to get a read on what was going through her mind. Her emotions were closed to me and I was at a total loss as to how she felt.

I used the ride to think about the upcoming week. Tomorrow I would go back to work, get behind the wheel of the truck, and run my route like I had been doing for the past three years. My job was how I had met Celeste, but it was also how I had met Ebonie. Life had a way of putting you in the craziest situations, but at the end of the day, it was all about how you handled them. I knew that I had to make things right with Celeste, and I was going to do just that. I was not going to waste this opportunity that we had to make our marriage work. We still had a long way to go to sort through all of the things that had happened but I knew we could do it.

As we rolled along in the shuttle, I took my phone out of my pocket and powered up the device. It had been buried in my suitcase for the past few days, and I absentmindedly scrolled through all of the emails, notifications, and texts that flooded the phone the instant I turned it back on. I froze with shock the instant I came across one text message in particular.

Ebonie: Hello

I stared at the inauspicious, one-word message for several minutes. She had never contacted me before. Why now? Was something wrong with Imani? My mind raced as I tried to process all of the possible implications of her message which was sent two days ago according to the time stamp.

Celeste, who was sitting across from me on the opposite bench seat, must have seen the emotions on my face because she asked, "Is everything okay, Dante?"

Her soft tone jolting me back to reality, I looked up at her, suddenly feeling a sense of peace. This was something that I had not felt in a long time.

"Yeah, love," I answered in a reassuring tone, leaning forward, reaching across the aisle and taking her hand in mine. "Everything is just fine."

I didn't know what Ebonie wanted, but I was sure that I would find out soon enough. She could wait however. Right now, I had to focus on my wife. Things between us were my top priority. It wouldn't be easy, by no stretch of the imagination, but I knew that Celeste and I would make it. I loved my wife and even though I had made a horrible decision, if Celeste would stay by my side, I would make sure that she would know just how much she meant to me.

30

Michal

I was barely aware of the people rushing around me, all of the travelers going in and out of the airport terminal. They were virtually invisible as my body and brain felt like they were both a few stages away from shutting down. I had only gotten less than three hours of sleep after having been up all day, and fatigue was finally catching up with me.

The normally deafening rumble of aircraft engines powering up on the runway a few hundred feet from where I stood was almost imperceptible as I sat outside of the airport waiting for my ride to pick me up. Physically, I was there, but my mind, my heart, was all hundreds of miles away.

The past several hours consisted of me going through a gauntlet of shuttles, planes, and long lines, but all of that was finally behind me. Now here I was, flanked by a large suitcase and carry-on bag as I sat in front of George Bush Intercontinental Airport, back in Houston after a truly unforgettable vacation.

The time spent with my girls was something I would hold dear until the next time that we all were able to get together. Darlene was supposed to have been there with us on the cruise, having fun, soaking up the sun, enjoying her life, but instead, she was gone. Forever.

Darlene's unexpected death illustrated in dramatic fashion how short life was. I once again contemplated the fact that each day that you are blessed to wake up and draw breath, should be lived to the fullest. With that sobering thought in mind, it made it that much more difficult to know that I would have to wait another two years before I could let Desiré come out to play again. Should I let her out sooner?

As that question permeated my thoughts, my mind drifted to the many things that I had done on the cruise. Those pleasant thoughts turned dark as the painful memory of my confrontation with Kendra came rushing to the forefront. For almost the entire cruise, she had been making all sorts of snide comments under her breath. It wasn't until this morning, however, that things finally came to a head.

I had been in my own little world, staring out of the window in our room, watching as the ship slowly made its way back in to Miami.

Kendra was sitting on her bed scrolling through pictures from the weekend on her tablet. Out of the blue, she put the device down and asked in a tone brimming with animosity, "You know it's really foul what you're doing, right?"

Her words settled in the quiet room as I turned away from the window to her, not really knowing what she was talking about or what she meant by her question. I tried once again to understand where the anger was coming from, but again, I could not cite the source. Whatever her reasons were, I knew she had a lot more to say and that it was way past the time for us to have this conversation.

"Don't act like you don't know what I'm talking about," she said derisively, getting up from the bed, coming to stand beside me. Rather than looking outside through the thick, sea-stained glass, she instead kept her gaze focused squarely on me.

"No, I really don't have a clue," I said, getting annoyed with both her behavior and her questions.

Who in the hell did she think she was to judge me? I thought, still trying to figure out just what her issue was with me. Even though we had been friends for years, I was confident she didn't know everything that she thought she did.

"But even if I did, why exactly does what I do or don't do even matter to you?" I asked, trying to keep my tone even and my annoyance with her in check.

"It does matter to me!" she spat. "You've got what every woman is dreaming of and yet you risk it all. And for what? A few cheap thrills? You're damn right it matters to me."

The sudden rage that seemed to surge through her as she spoke caused me to take a small step back. In that instant, her mood seemed to change, her posture relaxed and her voice took on such a pained tone, surprising me even more than her angry outburst had.

"You don't have a problem getting men," she said with a hint of disdain. "You didn't have any problem back in college getting with getting with Darlene's man, Owen."

My heart skipped a beat at the mention of Owen's name. I had no idea anyone knew about the clandestine relationship he and I had all those years ago back in school. I thought it was a secret that went with him to his grave, but here she was, shattering that fragile idea with the power of her words.

"Look, Kendra, I don't know what you're talking about," I said, my voice cracking as I tried futilely to stall for time. I needed to gather my thoughts and recover from the emotional curveball she had just thrown at me.

"Please! Don't even try that. I know all about you and Owen," she snapped, her body tensing as the anger returned with full force. "And please don't tell me I didn't see what I saw you doing in Vegas."

"You saw me? Oh my God!" I gasped, trying unsuccessfully to hide the shock at hearing her reveal this to me.

"Yes, I saw you," she answered simply, quietly. Her body once again relaxed as she turned away from me and looked out the window. The skyline of Miami in the distance created a postcard worthy picture through the glass, but I could tell Kendra was not focused on any of that.

I closed my eyes. My shoulders slumped as all of the fight drained out of me. I recalled all of the things that I'd done in

Vegas. I couldn't believe anyone, let alone one of my longtime girlfriends, would ever know about my late night activities in Sin City. I thought I was being so careful in keeping my secret moves hidden from everyone but obviously that wasn't the case.

"You remember that Saturday night in Vegas, don't you?" she asked as she turned directly at me, arms crossed over her chest, her pose a challenge, daring me to deny anything that she was saying.

"Saturday night?" I asked, turning away from her so I could avoid meeting her rancor. Out of the corner of my eye, I could see she was waiting on a response.

I knew exactly what she was referring, but I still held out hope that maybe she was wrong. Finally, I turned to her and said simply, "Yes, I remember that we all hung out on Saturday. I remember going to the Lion King musical at Mandalay Bay. Then we went back to the hotel, ate dinner, and then turned in for the rest of the night. There wasn't much more to it than that."

"Not much more? Yeah, right." she sneered, rolling her eyes dramatically. "Sure, we did go back to the hotel. That's about the only truthful thing that you've said. Please cut out the lies and half-truths and just be honest for once in your life!"

"Whatever, Kendra," I said, using bravado to camouflage my growing anxiety. "It was two years ago. I can't remember exactly what happened every second of that trip."

"Oh, really? You don't remember the guy that had you calling for Jesus as he had you bent over behind that car?" she asked, laughing mockingly. "In the hotel parking garage? Any of that ring a bell? Do you remember now"

I was stunned to hear her talk about my hedonistic hunts that I engaged in while we were in Vegas. I dropped my head and let out a defeated sigh, the memory of that night vividly coming back to me. I couldn't believe it. *How could I have been so sloppy?* I thought, mentally kicking myself. I had too much to lose if what I had done was to ever get out.

My sexual safaris were my release in every sense of the word. Whether they want to admit it or not, the truth is that everyone has a vice. Be it drugs, gambling, alcohol, shopping, you name it, someone uses it for a release. I was no different than anyone else in that I had a secret vice and if those that I cared about the most were to ever find out, my whole world as I knew it would crumble.

"I don't know why you do the things you do," she said, closing her toiletries bag. "No matter how hard I try, I'll never be able to understand why you're willing to throw away everything you have. You're right though. All of that isn't my concern. You're grown, so I guess you can do what you want, no matter how messed up it might be."

She was right, I did do what I wanted to do. What she didn't realize was how hard it was to have desires that you couldn't act upon for a host of reasons. She could never know what it was like to essentially have to cut off a part of yourself and to not be who you really are. She would never understand the societal pressures I had to live with on a daily basis.

"What really pisses me off is that I want to be like you," she continued, the irony of her situation illustrated by the sad smile on her face. "Don't get it twisted though. I don't want to be a hoe and a housewife, but I do know I wanted more. I wanted to look better. To feel better. As I watched you and him, that's all I could think about. I decided right then and there I was going to do just that. The minute I got back to Corpus, I hired a personal trainer, got in the gym, and the results are what you see in front of you."

The silence that filled the room was intense as we both digested this shared secret. She took a deep breath and continued, "You have it all, girl. You have the things I could only dream about. I lost the weight, so all that's missing now is a husb—"

"Michal! Hey, baby," a familiar male voice said, interrupting my thoughts, quickly snapping me back to the present. I stood up from the railing I had been leaning on and faced the man speaking to me. The man that I hadn't seen in five days. The man that I had been married to for the last ten years.

"Hey, boo," I said, standing to my feet and going over to greet my husband. "I missed you so much, Brian."

I embraced my college sweetheart who later became my spouse, holding him, squeezing him, exchanging a deep kiss, our lips connecting, our spirits reconnecting after being away from each other for the better part of a week. I loved this man more than anything in the world. I held him tight, enjoying the feeling of absolute security that came every time he wrapped his arms around me. True, he didn't have the chiseled body of a male underwear model, but he was my thick teddy bear and I loved every inch of him. With his deep brown skin, tall stature, neat appearance, and mature self-confidence, he was an African king to me. His calm demeanor, caring personality, the perpetual smile that always seemed to be in place, all made me fall in love with him each time I saw him.

Breaking our embrace, he went over to pick up my luggage and dutifully took them to the open hatch of our burgundy colored SUV. As he was doing this, I opened up the rear passenger-side door and was greeted to the shrill chorus of "MOMMY!" that came from my two children seated in the back.

I reached inside the car and hugged Anise, my 7-year-old daughter, who was strapped into her seatbelt, her little arms locking around my neck in a tight bear hug. I pulled free from her and reached over to hug Michael, my 5-year-old son who was securely buckled in his booster seat. I hugged them both, my heart swelling with happiness and I fought to hold back tears of joy at being back home with my family.

I climbed into the front passenger seat through the door he held open for me. It felt so good to be home, to be with my husband, to be with my children.

"So how was the trip?" Brian asked after he got in behind the wheel, pulled away from curb, and smoothly merged into the busy airport traffic.

"It was great!" I responded enthusiastically. I proceeded to tell him about the tours, the excursions, the activities on the cruise ship, the fabulous dinners and all of the other wonderful things we had done.

I also told him about Darlene's demise and the tragic events surrounding her death. He listened quietly as I recounted her shooting Walter before being killed in the car accident.

A few silent moments passed before he finally spoke. "Damn! That's messed up," he said simply as he slowly shook his head in disbelief, a sad expression on his face. "I've never hidden the fact that I didn't like for Darlene, but I hate to hear that she died. I know it was way in the past, but I still can't get over what she did to Owen and almost did to me. If it wasn't for her funky attitude, we all would've been in our dorm room instead of out in the streets. She was the reason that Owen left his dorm the night that he was shot by the cops. We all could've ended up like him because of her. Anyway, like I said, that's in the past. I don't even want to think about all that."

"Yeah, me either," I said quietly, reaching over to gently rub his leg. As we drove on the outer loop on the way to our home in Baytown, I looked out the window, trying to force back the memories of those tumultuous times back at Texas Southern. "Enough sad stuff. Anyway, what about you. What did you guys get into while I was gone? Did y'all miss me?" I said, turning to my kids in the back seat.

"Yes, Mommy," they answered in unison. I listened as they told me about the adventures they went on with their dad, from going to Chuck E. Cheese's to them going on a tour of the Space Center.

"I wanna be an ashro-not," Michael said happily.

"You do?" I responded with a giggle, thoroughly loving my cute little boy.

"Man, I'm so glad you're back," Brian said with a chuckle. "I'm exhausted. Those two ran me ragged."

"Oh really?" I asked, giving his thigh a slap. "You mean to tell me that you can't handle two kids for five days?"

"Ow! I didn't say all that," he said, a big grin on his face. "I'm just saying that you are way better at it than I am. Hell, you get paid to handle kids."

"And I have the rest of the week off," I said, slapping his thigh again. "School is out this week. We're still on Thanksgiving holiday, remember?"

"Ow! Quit it," he said, laughing as he rubbed the spot where I hit him. "Yeah, I remember. How could I forget?"

"For the rest of the week, Michal is still on vacation," I said. "I'll go back to being Mrs. Sexton on Monday."

As a third grade teacher at Brown Elementary in the Houston Independent School District, I not only had to deal with all of my students, but their parents, the school's principal, and everyone in between. I loved my job, but Lord knows it was a stressful one and one of many reasons I was so glad to have this much needed time off.

It was also one of the justifications that I used for my periodic escapes in which I allowed Desiré to come free. Kendra alluded earlier this morning that I lived what a lot of people would consider to be the perfect life. I was the wife to a handsome, loving husband who was a deacon of our church, and a mother to two beautiful, intelligent children. I was a third grade elementary school teacher with my sights set on one day becoming a principal at one of the schools in the district. Because of those reasons and many more, I had to control when and where Desiré surfaced. I thought back to my conversation with Kendra this morning and was once again haunted by her words. I had too much to lose if Desiré was to ever come out at the wrong time or if the wrong person found out about her.

The last few days was my time to let her out, to fill my needs, to satisfy my desires. The cruise was over now and with that, it was time for Desiré to go back into the deep recesses of my mind and body where she dwelled, dormant until the next time that she could be released to come out and play.

I watched the scenery rush by through the clear glass of the window. I thought about how I was now returning to my normal life. Returning to being a wife and mother at home and a teacher and colleague at work.

I stared off into the distance and thought about the future and what it held. Another two years until we would be going south of the border to Mexico for our next girlfriend getaway. *There is that one particular resort I have wanted to check out for a while now. Let the countdown to temptation in Cancun begin,* I thought as a sly smile spread across my face.

The End

Made in the USA
Columbia, SC
17 May 2019